OPERATION COBRA

Also by Anders Bodelsen

ANDERS BODELSON

OPERATION COBRA

Translated by Joan Tate

ELSEVIER/NELSON BOOKS

NEW YORK

First published in the U.S.A. (1979) by Elsevier/Nelson Books, a division of Elsevier-Dutton Publishing Company, Inc., New York.

Library of Congress Cataloging in Publication Data

Bodelsen, Anders.
    Operation Cobra.

    SUMMARY: Three young boys realize they have witnessed the beginnings of a plot to assassinate the American Secretary of State during his visit to Copenhagen.
    [1. Terrorosm—Fiction.   2. Denmark—Fiction]
I. Title.
PZ7.B635170p 1979   [Fic]   79-16564
ISBN 0-525-66652-4

Printed in the U.S.A.   First edition
10 9 8 7 6 5 4 3 2 1

OPERATION COBRA

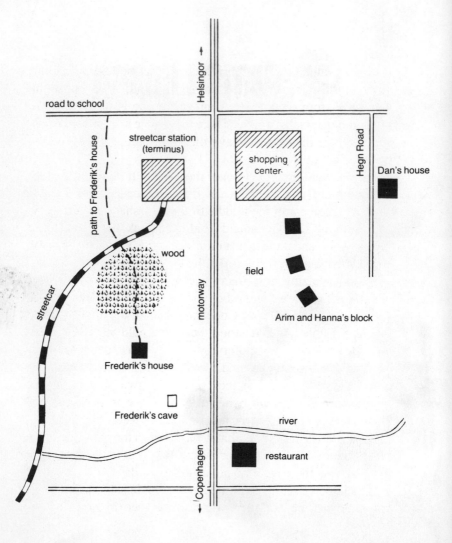

MONDAY

1

Dan was standing on the bridge over the motorway, looking down at the cars. He had his bag in his hand, as he was on his way back from school. He weighed the bag in his hand. How much did it actually weigh? There were quite a lot of books in it, and some of them were heavy ones. Dan thought that the bag weighed about five kilos.

He was holding the bag over the railing. If he let it go at the right moment, it would hit a car. If he practiced a little, he could probably hit a car in the middle of the windshield. What would happen then? The windshield would not break, but it would turn milky white, and if the driver didn't have the presence of mind to knock the glass out with his fist, he would have to steer blind.

It was amazing how many accidents you could cause and which for some reason or other you didn't, thought Dan.

The cars coming from Copenhagen were mostly driving as fast as possible. As Dan stood there, he could see as far as the next bridge over the motorway, which was four kilometers away. He had good eyes and spotted a green sports car passing under the next bridge. It took just about two minutes for the green sports car to pass beneath Dan, so it was driving at 120 kilometers per hour, ten more than was allowed.

Dan lifted up his bag so that it was back on the right side of the railing again. It was lucky for the man in the green sports car, he thought, that there were no police around today.

He sauntered on, in no particular hurry. He hadn't arranged to play with anyone, and there was no one expecting him at home, because neither his father nor his mother would be back until just before they were to have their meal. Dan was an only child and at the moment he had no special friends where he lived on Hegn Road.

His best friends were two boys in his class, with whom he had walked most of the way home. Arim had hurried on, because he was going to fly kites with some others Dan didn't know. Dan had told Arim that there wasn't really enough wind, but at the moment Arim was so crazy about kites that he didn't mind whether it was good kite weather or not.

Arim was also crazy about his new friends, who had discarded the kind of kites you bought in shops and instead made their own, which they said flew much better. Dan thought that flying kites was kid stuff, but at the same time he thought it might be great to be in on making a really big kite yourself.

The other friend who had been with him was called Frederik. Frederik had to go home with his small sister, which was why he had already left them before they got to the bridge. Frederik's father was a forest ranger and they lived in an isolated house. Frederik's small sister, Margrethe, went to the same school as Dan, Arim, and Frederick, but three grades below them, and she wasn't allowed to go home on her own. So Frederik had to go with her, which neither of them liked very much.

On the corner of Hegn Road, by the telephone booth, a taxi was standing with the door to the driver's seat open and the engine running. The door of the booth was open too. The taxi driver was standing there, hunting through his pockets. When he caught sight of Dan, he said:

"Can you change a five-kroner note?"

Dan rummaged through his own pockets. He had had a ten-kroner note with him that morning, but he'd spent seven kroner and had only three left.

"All right, I'll take them," said the taxi driver. "Then you'll have made a nice profit."

Dan stood there with the five-kroner note in his hand. The taxi driver dropped the coins into the pay phone and stood tapping his foot on the ground as he waited to get through. He was wearing a very large, flashy watch which Dan thought he'd like to have a closer look at. It appeared to be both a watch and an alarm clock. The call came through, and before the taxi driver closed the door, Dan noticed that he was speaking English.

In the meantime, there was something else that had attracted Dan's attention. The taxi's engine was running. It was a Mercedes. Dan knew enough about cars to know that it did not sound like a diesel engine. This made him walk around behind the car to see what was on the back, and to his astonishment he saw that it said "240 D" in chrome letters on the back plate.

D stood for diesel, but Dan was a hundred percent sure that a diesel engine didn't sound like that. When he looked closer, he also noticed that there were *two* exhaust pipes. So it was even more unbelievable that it was a diesel engine, because they never had more than one exhaust pipe. He went around to the front of the vehicle and listened to the engine. No doubt about it, it was a gasoline engine and it also sounded like a very large one. More likely a six-cylinder than a four-cylinder. In fact, Dan wouldn't have been surprised if there had been eight cylinders under the hood.

The taxi driver came out of the telephone booth, looked at his big watch and hurried across to the vehicle.

"Why does it say diesel on the back?" Dan asked.

"Because it is a diesel," said the taxi driver.

"But that's a gasoline engine. I can hear that," said Dan.

The taxi driver was staring at his watch.

"No," he said. "It's a diesel, as it says."

"Then why are there two exhaust pipes?" Dan asked.

The driver stopped looking at his watch and looked at Dan. He seemed to think for a moment before replying.

"I can't imagine. There should be."

"No," said Dan, as definitely as he could. "There shouldn't."

"Oh, well," said the driver, getting in, slamming the door and revving up. The engine accelerated faster and more silently than any diesel engine would, and there was not a trace of diesel smoke from either of the two exhaust pipes. It also looked as if the vehicle hung a little differently from the way a taxi usually does.

That was pretty extraordinary, thought Dan. A Mercedes taxi with a gasoline engine, and a driver who either doesn't know it or else is lying.

The only thing Dan was certain of was that he hadn't been mistaken. He walked the last bit of the way home, kicking himself for not having taken down the number. That was indeed a rarity.

2

Arim, Dan's school friend, and two other boys from the same block were trying to get a kite up, one they'd finished making the evening before. It was a large cross-kite, seventy centimeters wide and over a meter long. Arim's mother had helped them with the sewing. The material was yellow linen, which made the kite easy to see, even when it was flying very high up.

The three boys went to the best place they knew to get the kite up—the long slope that ran from the shopping center down to the river, where there were neither buildings nor trees to take away the wind, and the slope was sufficient for them to get up a good speed before letting the kite go. The problem today was that it wasn't very windy. The wind was indeed coming from the south, in from Copenhagen, but there wasn't much of it, and it kept dropping.

As the kite was quite big, it was also heavy, and they couldn't get if off the ground. At first the other two boys ran with it, and then Arim had a try to see if he could run faster or have a bit better luck. He ran as fast as he could down the slope toward the river, and when he was quite certain he couldn't run any faster, he let the kite go. The other two stood holding the line, which was rolled up on a spindle of the kind Arim's father used when he went out fishing.

For a moment it looked as if Arim had had better luck than the other two. The yellow kite rose five or six meters above the ground, flapped a bit in the wind, looked like it was getting the wind under it and flying, but then the wind suddenly dropped and let the kite go, and it fell almost vertically straight down onto the grass. When the boys went to pick it up, they found that one of the cross sticks had broken. There would be no more flying the kite that afternoon.

After agreeing to meet to repair the kite, they went back the way they had come. In front of them lay the shopping center, with its view over the field. To the left ran the motorway, always noisy, but especially so in the afternoon when people were driving home out of town. To the right lay the apartment houses where Arim and his friends lived. The other two took a shortcut through to get home, but Arim decided to go and look in the toy store to see if they'd got one of those little plastic kites which he could fly just once before going home to do his homework.

The woman in the toy store got out three different kites, all three of them under ten kroner. None of them looked much good, but all the same, Arim was able to stand and look at them for a while, as some other customers came into the shop and the woman went off to wait on them.

After Arim had stood there looking at the three plastic kites for a while, he began to listen to what the new customers were talking about to the woman. They were two men, and they could only speak English. The woman didn't understand English, and

Arim wondered whether it would be conceited of him if he started helping her. He had taken English at school for three years and could understand most of what the men were saying. They wanted a toy for a girl of about six or seven, they said.

The woman couldn't make out what they were talking about, so in the end Arim shoved the plastic kites to one side and went to help the two Englishmen and the woman to understand each other. The two men bought a large, hideous doll, which closed its eyes when you laid it down and opened them and said ma-ma when you stood it up again.

The woman looked at Arim and shook her head with a smile. Arim smiled back. Suddenly, one of the Englishmen caught sight of a mask that was hanging in the carnival-costume department. He tried it on and looked disappointed, because it was much too small for him. The other man also began to play with the masks. The two men wanted to know if the women had one in their size. Arim translated as best he could. The woman shook her head. She didn't think they had fancy masks for adults, but she went over to the two men to help them look.

One of them had found a black mask which covered only the eyes. It wasn't for an adult, but he just managed to get it on. He laughed as he tried it on, but the other man didn't laugh and in the end it seemed almost as if the two were quarreling. The laughing man swiftly removed the mask and stopped grinning when he saw how angry the other one was. Arim glanced at the angry one and wondered why he behaved like that just because his friend was playing with a mask that was too small for him.

The Englishmen decided to buy the doll only and then they left the store. Outside, just before the door closed, Arim heard one of them laugh again and saw the other one shove him irritably aside.

"What a strange pair," said the woman.

Arim nodded.

"Thanks for your help," the woman said to him. "You certainly do learn English at school. Well, do you want one of the kites?"

Arim shook his head.

"You can have one for five kroner, for helping me," the woman said.

So Arim bought a plastic kite after all, and a moment or so later he was down on the slope in front of the shopping center again, and the kite did actually fly, although there wasn't any wind. But he had to run fast to keep it up, and it wouldn't have been true to say that it flew especially well.

It was growing dark when Arim stopped, out of breath. He could hardly see the kite any longer, although it wasn't all that high up. There were lots of cars on their way out of town now, and, on the other side of the motorway, he saw the streetcar coming along, the lights on in its windows.

On his way home, he thought about the two strange Englishmen in the toy store. What did they want with that large doll, and why had one of them suddenly got so angry about the other fooling around with a mask that didn't fit him?

When the man who hadn't laughed had paid for the doll, Arim had noticed his wallet—it was made of something that looked like alligator skin, and it was very fat. There had been many more five-hundred kroner notes than the one the man had paid with, and for which the woman in the shop had had trouble giving change.

3

Frederik, who was in Dan and Arim's class, was cycling home with his sister, Margrethe. When he was with the other two, he made it quite clear that he didn't like looking after his sister. But when he was alone with her, they got on quite well together. Frederik understood perfectly well why his parents thought he should take Margrethe home from school, because although the Poulsen family didn't live all that far away from other people, they did live in a very isolated place.

The two of them cycled first along the road that ran behind the end station of the streetcar line and some new apartment houses. There was quite a bit of traffic on this stretch. But then the road crossed the rails and from then on vanished into the woods, which was part of the area where their father was forest ranger.

In the summer, lots of people went along this road, as it led to a large camping site near the motorway. But now, in February, you could ride all the way home without meeting anyone else at all, and the part through the woods was quite dark. You could hear the sound of traffic from the motorway all the time, but you couldn't see the cars, and neither could you be seen from them.

As she tried to keep up with Frederik, Margrethe chattered breathlessly on about her costume for next Monday, on the carnival holiday. Frederik didn't like getting into costume and shaking a collecting box any longer, but as he had to go with Margrethe, he might just as well talk to her about it.

She had got it into her head that she wanted to be an African. Not just on her face, but also on her neck and hands. She wanted her mother to help with a real afro haircut, and then she thought she wouldn't need a mask to be unrecognizable.

"Who are you going to collect for?" asked Frederik.

"Myself," said Margrethe, pedaling hard to keep up with him. "Who else?"

She was surprisingly good at keeping up with him, even when he really put a spurt on.

"Vietnam or Bangladesh . . ."

Frederik couldn't think for a moment of any other place where they needed money and ended up saying: "Or the Red Cross."

Margrethe exploited the fact that Frederik had stopped pedaling as he tried to think of a third place to collect money for, and caught right up with him.

The last stretch of the wood was quite dark. Here the trees were closer to the road and most of them were conifers. When Frederik rode home alone at night, he was usually very pleased when he got to the end of the road and caught sight of the house, where the lights were always on in the barn entrance and above the front door, because Frederik and Margrethe's mother was a bit afraid of the dark.

The Poulsens' house lay on the edge of the wood where the camping site was. In the summer there could be as many as several thousand campers and their cars and tents and trailers on the site, but from October to April, it was closed. While Frederik and Margrethe's father looked after the forest behind their house all year round, their mother ran the camping site in the summer. In the winter she was "just a housewife," as she put it.

The forester's house lay well hidden by some trees, which their mother had often said should be felled to let in more sun. Behind the house, the forest began, and on the other side there was a large open space down to the motorway. There was no fence to show where the garden really stopped, and in that way the garden and the open space you could play in was as large as you wanted it to be.

When the house came into view, Frederik put on a spurt, as

now he was certainly going to show that he could ride faster than his sister, but to his annoyance, he found he couldn't shake her off. He arrived home first, but she was hard on his heels, and they were both almost equally out of breath.

Ringo, their dog, ran out to meet them. He was a golden retriever and shared his affections equally between Frederik and Margrethe. He was supposed to be a guard dog and bark at strangers, but he was just as enthusiastic about all company and frightened no one away.

Mrs. Poulsen opened the door and Anisette, the cat, slipped out. She wasn't afraid of Ringo either, but the Poulsens had acquired the dog and the cat at the same time and brought them up together, so they were good friends and ate out of the same bowl. When Frederik and Margrethe squabbled, Mrs. Poulsen said they had a lot to learn from Ringo and Anisette.

Frederik went out into the kitchen and picked up the open sandwich which his mother had spread for him. Now that he had accompanied his sister home and even talked to her, he wanted to be alone. He didn't take his overcoat off, but quickly drank a glass of milk his mother had poured for him and went out into the garden again.

His mother looked as if she had hoped he would sit down for a while and tell her what he'd done at school that day, but she would have to make do with Margrethe today. Ringo followed Frederik as he went out with his sandwich in his hand.

Frederik walked down toward the motorway, following a narrow path at first, then continuing between some fir trees to a cave he had been working on lately, and which he had almost finished the day before.

The cave was among some fir trees behind a hillock, and from the hillock an open stretch of heath ran down to the motorway. You couldn't see the cars from the cave, but you could hear them, of course.

There had been a hole between the trees before, but Frederik had borrowed a spade without asking and dug the hole deeper. Then he had found large branches that had fallen from the trees, and also a few boards left over from when his father had built a shed in the autumn. He had placed these over the hole, so that it had become a cave. The previous day, he had camouflaged the cave by placing some pine branches right across the opening and the roof. You would have to know that the cave was there, or stand very close to it, to be able to see it.

Frederik turned around, because he saw that Ringo was lagging farther behind than he usually did. He whistled to him and waited for him to come rushing up, but it was quite a time before he did, and when he finally appeared, he had his nose to the ground as if he had got scent of something or other. Probably a fox, thought Frederik, patting Ringo, who was looking very excited, and seemed to want to run back and sniff again at the scent he had found.

After Frederik had been down into the cave and ensured that his flashlight and box of provisions—cookies and chocolate— were where they should be, he came up and covered up the entrance again. Ringo had not been down in the cave, but when he saw Frederik, he ran over to him and looked at him, then turned back again and kept looking to see if he was following. He was.

Ringo ran across the open stretch of heath which lay between the cave and the motorway, constantly turning to make sure that Frederik was following him. Suddenly he stopped just below the high-tension wires, sniffing at something he had found, his tail wagging madly. Frederik bent down to see what it was he was being so enthusiastic about.

At first it looked like a withered yellow birch leaf. But then he realized that it was some kind of negative of a film. It took him a while to get it out of Ringo's mouth. He looked at it more closely. The negative was faded and he could no longer see what it was of. On the back of it was printed "Polaroid." It must have been thrown there by a camper in the summer. But it was strange that Ringo had snapped it up so eagerly, as if it had a fresh scent on it.

Ringo ran up onto the embankment of the motorway, where he stopped with his nose to the ground. Frederik went up to him to see what it was that was still exciting him so much.

Frederik tired of sharing Ringo's enthusiasm and looked up instead. High up in the sky, he spotted something yellow. It was quite a time before he saw that it was a kite, and it was even longer before he realized that it must be the kite Arim had told him about at school that day. Frederik glanced down, and after looking across at the slope in front of the shopping center on the other side of the motorway for a while, he spotted three small dots, which were probably Arim and his friends. One of the three was running very fast to get the kite up, but when Frederik looked up toward the kite again, he saw that it was coming down.

Arim's kite reminded Frederik that he must take the flashlight back home with him from the cave. It was an extra-powerful one which he'd got for Christmas, and it had a red and a green light, as well as a white one. Arim had been given one just like it, and they had practiced signaling to each other. The two boys could see each other's windows, although there was a whole kilometer between them.

With the flashlight in his hand, Frederik walked back home. Ringo was still behaving in a peculiar way. He was unwilling to go home, and kept sniffing at the ground, barking at Frederik as he drew away from him. He had never behaved like that before.

Arim's father was a photographer, Frederik remembered. When the opportunity arose, he would ask him how that kind of Polaroid camera really worked.

4

Dan was alone at home and was feeling rather bored, looking out of the kitchen window and thinking that nothing ever happened in Narum, and nothing ever happened especially on Hegn Road.

He had heard someone say that Hegn Road was the "best" road in Narum, and perhaps it was, but it wasn't especially lively, no interesting cars drove along it, and not many people he wanted to be with lived there. Both Dan's father and mother worked away from home most of the day, his father as a doctor at a hospital, his mother as a librarian. Dan had once asked why he was an only child, and his father had said:

"Don't you think there are enough children in the world?"

There was no answer to that, Dan had thought.

It would be a couple of hours before his parents would get back home and he would have to help lay the table and so on, so Dan wandered around looking for something to make the time pass. Of course, he had homework for tomorrow, but he figured on doing that in his free periods.

The morning paper was lying in the living room and he started looking at the front page. It was a thin little newspaper his parents took, with hardly any pictures in it, and only one cartoon strip. Well, he could read an article without pictures, couldn't he? Dan started reading a long article about the Middle East crisis.

War was brewing up down there again, between Israel and the Arab countries. Dan was a Jewish name. Most people thought it was a very Danish name, but it stemmed from the Old Testament Dan, one of the sons of Jacob and Billah, and there was a whole Jewish tribe descended from him, Dan's father had told him.

19

Dan's father was Jewish and had had to move to Sweden during the German occupation of Denmark. Dan's mother wasn't Jewish, and in that way Dan was a "half-Jew."

Half-Jew, Dan said to himself, abandoning the long newspaper article on the war in the Middle East. For fun, he added "half-Dane." He had tried that once when his father had been listening and his father had hurried to correct him. "No," he'd said. "You're wholly Danish, and so am I—and so is your mother, of course."

Half-Jew, thought Dan. Wholly Danish. Peculiar words.

His friend Arim was a half-Dane, wasn't he? Or wholly Danish? Arim's father had been born in Tunisia and had come to Denmark as an adult, where he had married Arim's mother, who was wholly Danish. Arim had an elder sister, whom they had called Hanna in a wholly Danish way. Later on Arim had arrived, and he had been given a name which as far as Dan knew was wholly Tunisian.

Dan got up, abandoning the newspaper, and, bored, wandered around. He stopped by the record player, but he didn't feel like listening to his own records today, and his parents had stopped buying decent records after the Beatles. He couldn't bear to listen to them anyhow, so he went into his room, where he read a boring old back number of a horror comic.

It was all about some vampires in a castle in the Middle Ages, or something, and it was too long ago, or perhaps too distant. Most exciting of all, thought Dan, were really the things that went on on television, things you sat and watched while they were going on. Like boxing matches and football matches, and that time on Swedish television when they'd shown some real bank robbers, who had held several people hostage in a bank in the middle of Stockholm.

Dan walked back across the dining room and again looked at the newspaper with the long article on the crisis in the Middle

East. Obviously another war was brewing up, and it was the very last moment if there was to be any mediation. Dan was on the Israelis' side, like most Danes. And his father had also said that "we're on the Israelis' side, *because* we're Danish and democratic."

At school, Dan had also felt that they were all in favor of the Israelis, just as they obviously were on the television news. All except one of their teachers, who had taken up a whole lesson telling them about the crisis in the Middle East. Although he had taken pains to explain what things looked like for both the Israelis and the Arabs, Dan had sensed that the teacher mostly favored the Arabs.

Dan thought about Arim. Arim's father was Tunisian, and Tunisia was a member of the Arab bloc. He hadn't thought about that before. If Arim thought in any way differently about the Middle East at school, then he kept it to himself.

Dan went into his room for the second time, pushed the horror comic to one side and started hunting for something; some car brochures he had been given at a motor show. *Given* was perhaps not quite the right word. He had taken them when the salesman had been looking in another direction. He found some fat colorful brochures advertising Mercedes cars.

He sought out the brochure for the model which was also used as a taxi. He had remembered quite correctly. If there were *two* exhaust pipes behind, then it was because there was at least a six-cylinder gasoline engine in it, which gave the vehicle a top speed of almost two hundred kilometers an hour.

Dan had forgotten all about half-Jews and half-Danes and half-Arabs and the crisis in the Middle East. He sat there thinking about the taxi driver who had lied and about a taxi that looked just like any other taxi, but which in all likelihood would be able to go at up to two hundred kilometers an hour!

21

5

Arim was having his evening meal with his parents and his elder sister, Hanna. The Hafsid family ate alternatively Tunisian and Danish food, because Arim's father was Tunisian and his mother Danish.

Arim's father had come to Denmark as a photographer working for an international agency, and then he had met Arim's mother and settled in Denmark. He still worked for an international agency, but only part time. For the rest of the time, he worked for himself and took the photographs that he wanted to take. For several years he had been working on a large picture book which was to show what Denmark was like, as seen through a stranger's eyes.

"The trouble is," he would say now and again, "I no longer feel I am a stranger. I've begun to get used to what is nice as well as what is nasty."

During dinner, Arim tried to tell his sister and his parents about the peculiar experience he had had in the toy store, but Hanna interrupted him.

"You're just telling us that to boast that you're better at speaking English than the woman in the toy store," she said.

That shut Arim up, because it wasn't far from the truth.

Hanna was talking to her father. She had recently been given a camera, and now she was always talking about cameras and photography with her father; she was allowed to go into her father's darkroom.

Arim had been allowed in there once or twice, but then he'd happened to switch on a light by mistake, and his father had been so angry that he'd gone over to Arabic, which Arim hardly understood, in order to tell him just how quickly he should get out of the room.

Arim's father had become rather more bad-tempered recently, which perhaps had something to do with Arim's mother being at home more than she used to be. Arim's father loved being alone at home in the mornings, while Arim and his sister were at school.

Arim's mother taught Danish to foreign workers from Arab countries. The trouble now was that Arab workers were becoming unemployed and being sent home, so Arim's mother was also unemployed. At one time she had worked full time, but now she only went into Copenhagen to teach for a couple of hours a week.

Arim helped his mother clear away. Hanna had helped her father cook the food and tomorrow it would be the other way around. Arim's father made plans for almost everything that happened in the household. Among other things, he had made a plan for who should go to the bathroom and when in the mornings. It was rather irritating as well as good fun with all those plans. They had one advantage, though, and that was that you weren't suddenly faced with something you didn't expect.

"Don't *you* think it was peculiar, that business with the two Englishmen buying a doll and trying on masks and then standing there squabbling in a toy store?" Arim asked his mother.

"Yes, I do," said his mother. "But hold the glasses up to the light before you put them away in the cupboard."

When the dishes had been washed and put away, Arim and his mother went in and watched television. Hanna and her father had vanished up to the attic, where a studio and a darkroom had been installed with the permission of all the other people in the building.

The television news was mostly about unemployment, and

23

Arim sat wondering what would happen if he went up to the attic and knocked on the door of the darkroom. Perhaps he'd be allowed in if he promised never to switch on a light again without thinking, and to be very careful not to knock over a bowl of developing liquid—he'd done that once, too.

Arim's birthday was in March, and he was hoping for a camera. But since neither his mother nor his father earned so much money now, he knew he could not count on getting a reflex camera like the one his sister had been given.

He had asked her once if he could borrow hers, but she had answered that she was afraid he would wreck it in four or five minutes. So now he had to hope for one of his own, and then they could no longer refuse him access to the darkroom.

On his way to his room, Arim passed the board on which his father had put some new photographs. One of them had been taken from the balcony facing the shopping center. Arim could see it had been taken to try out his father's newest and most powerful telescopic lens, because on the picture you could see only one single store—the radio store alongside the toy store, and the photograph was so sharp you could read the little signs in the window.

Arim went into his room. He put aside the little plastic kite which had turned out to fly so surprisingly well, and took out the homework he had to do for the next day. He heard his mother switch off the television and begin to type in the living room. She was translating a book about the Arab countries' view of the oil crisis and oil prices.

When Arim had looked at his school books for about ten minutes, he put them back into his schoolbag and took out another book which Frederik had borrowed for him from the library. In it was the Morse code. Frederik had gradually become angry with Arim, because he still didn't know it. This evening, Arim very much wanted to show Frederik that he really was learning it. He wanted to be able to send a whole word in

Morse with his flashlight, but which word was it to be? A short one, anyhow.

Arim thought that "bog" was a short word which he could learn by heart, but when you used Morse, you couldn't show that you were laughing at the same time, so perhaps he would have to find another one. "Hello" or "hi" were much too feeble, so finally he decided on "Dracula." Both Arim and Frederik were reading Dracula comics at present, so Frederik would understand what he meant.

Arim took his flashlight out and switched it on to see if it was a strong-enough light. He tried the red light, too, and the green one, then put out the light and tried "Dracula" in Morse on the wall.

The flashlight was the most powerful one you could get and weighed at least a kilo. But Arim reckoned it wouldn't be so difficult to use a smaller light up on a kite. That would be great at night. People would think it was a flying saucer or something.

You could use a kite to send something, too, he thought. If you were certain of the wind direction, you could send the kite up and let the line go. It would be great to send a written message over to Frederik, but it was probably pretty difficult to calculate the distance and the direction of the wind.

Just before nine o'clock, Arim opened the window to the balcony and climbed out through it. If he went through the living room and out through the balcony door, his mother would know what he was up to. It was four minutes to nine. He had checked his watch with the television.

As he was standing there, he could see right across the field that ran down to the river, and he could see the motorway, and behind the motorway, he could just see the dark forest. On the edge of the forest lay the Poulsens' house. A light was on on the ground floor, but not upstairs, where Frederik had his room.

That evening it was Frederik's turn to flash first, and Arim stood waiting for the first signal.

6

"Now we'll be really cozy," said Frederik's mother.

Not content with just turning off the television, she also pulled the plug out of the wall and gave the set on its wheels a push so that it slid away into the dark. Then she went out into the kitchen and brought back fruit and little cakes.

Frederik's father was kneeling in front of the fireplace, where he was stacking pieces of birchwood and lighting the fire. Ringo stood watching, his tail immobile, as the flames flared up, and then he turned back to the basket which he shared with Anisette. Anisette lay purring as Ringo carefully licked her neck.

"Aren't we nice and cozy?" said Frederik's mother.

Frederik's father and Margrethe said that they were, but Frederik sat wondering whether his father paid money to himself when he fetched a load of birch logs from the forest.

"Mother," said Margrethe. "Would you make me into an African?"

Her mother thought about it and then said that there was a week to go before carnival, but then she went out into the kitchen and came back with a cork, which she held in the flame of a candle. When the cork was black, she carefully blackened Margrethe's face. In the meantime, their father had lighted his pipe and when he went into his office, Frederik knew perfectly well what he was going to bring back and he thought: Oh, no. True enough, his father had his guitar with him when he reappeared. He sat down by the fire, tuned the guitar and began to play. Fortunately he didn't start singing, but Frederik knew that, in a little while, his mother would urge him to sing too, and she wouldn't find it difficult to persuade him.

Frederik knew all this only too well—the coziness, the fire-light, Anisette purring, the bowl of fruit, his father who was so easy to get to play and sing. But suddenly it was all too much for Frederik this evening. He sometimes thought his mother made them all cozy to order, and unlike Margrethe, who was being blackened into an African, he didn't seem to have a role to play in the coziness.

So when he had sat awhile and taken part in the coziness, he got up and said that he had some homework to do for the next day. His mother looked at him as if she didn't believe him, and as he was on his way upstairs, he heard his mother ask his father to sing something, and his father let himself be persuaded in less than a minute.

Up in his room, Frederik got a Vampirella comic out and read the last story he had left. He liked reading horrible things, but this story was almost too repulsive. It was about a woman who used to transform herself into a cat.

One morning, she finds a dead rat in her bedroom, and instead of being terrified of it, she sets about *eating* it. "The shock of the sight of the dead rat is almost immediately forgotten, and, as if in a trance, she goes over to the table." New picture. "And raises the rat carefully to her mouth . . . and bites." New picture. " . . . into it, so that the rodent's blood drips from her lips . . ." New picture. "But then . . ." New picture. "No, my God, what am I doing . . ." New picture. "I have GONE CRAZY . . . I am . . . I . . . I'm a . . ."

Ugh. It didn't make it any less horrible that the girl sitting there stuffing the rat into her mouth was quite pretty, with long blond hair and a very transparent dress.

Frederik closed the comic without finishing the story and sat listening to his father singing one of those Swedish songs he had sung a million times before. It was ten to nine, so Frederik got his flashlight and his binoculars out of his closet. It was easier for Arim to see Frederik's light than for Frederik to see Arim's. There were no other houses near Frederik's, only the dark forest and the camping site. And the Poulsens always drew their curtains in the evening.

Arim, on the other hand, lived in a block of apartment houses. The house faced the street, but not everyone drew their curtains and so you could easily be dazzled. To be certain of seeing Arim's light, Frederik used his father's old binoculars, which he held in his left hand while he held the flashlight in his right. Frederik moved the binoculars until he was certain he had them directed at Arim's balcony, which was easy to recognize, because the Christmas tree was still standing out on it.

There was a scratching at the door and a moment later, Ringo came in. That's another who's had enough coziness, thought Frederik. Ringo had seemed eager and excited ever since he'd been out to the cave that afternoon. Now he went over to the chair on which Frederik had hung his jacket and stood there sniffing, his tail up. After a while, he knocked the jacket onto the floor and tried to get his nose into the pocket.

What on earth was he up to? Frederik got up, but before he had got the jacket from the dog, Ringo had found something in the pocket—the negative he'd been so crazy about that afternoon.

Frederik tried to tease Ringo by taking the negative away from him, but for a change, Ringo growled and backed away. Well, he might as well keep the yellow bit of paper, thought Frederik. It was a minute to nine by his watch, which he had checked by the television, and he had to use both hands for the light and the binoculars.

He was to begin tonight, and on the dot of nine he flashed a green signal, which was always their starting signal.

Frederik's eyes were just getting used to the dark, and he thought he could just make out Arim's figure on the balcony on the other side of the motorway. Arim replied with three green signals.

Then came Frederik's personal recognition signal: white-red-white-green.

Frederik looked down at his list of signals and flashed green-green-green-white, which meant *I can see you clearly*. When there was damp in the air, it could be difficult for them to see each other, and sometimes it was impossible. Arim replied with the same signal. Then Frederik flashed: red-red-white-white. That meant: *Shall we go over to Morse?*

Arim's red-red-red meant *no*. Well, they could go on with agreed signals for a while. Arim's white-green-white meant *I'm fine*.

Oh, you are, are you? thought Frederik, signaling back that he was fine too. He suggested again with red-red-white-white, that they should practice Morse. Arim was darned dim about learning the Morse code.

Green-green-green replied Arim, which meant *yes*. After a pause, Arim began flashing lots of signals with the white light. Frederik had put down the binoculars. On the windowsill he had a pencil and a piece of paper for notes. As a sign that the message had ended, Arim flashed a red signal. Frederik replied again with six red signals and began to examine what he had written down.

Dim as he was, Arim had only signaled one word. The first letter was *D*, the next *R*, and the third *A*. But then there was a series of muddles and the only thing Frederik was certain of was that the word ended in *A* again.

Frederik flashed red-white-red-white, which meant *not understood*.

Arim repeated the same word. This time Frederik managed it better. *D-R-A*, then a letter he couldn't make out, then *U-L-A*.

Frederik guessed that the missing letter was a *C*. He shone the light once down onto his own Morse code and signaled back: *Vampirella*.

And then everything went wrong. Arim signaled *not understood* back, Frederik repeated *Vampirella* three times in a row, and finally he gave up using Morse altogether, and went over to the agreed signals with red and green again. Tomorrow, he would have to give Arim a real talking to, as it was no use if Frederik was the only one who knew the Morse code.

They both ended with white-white-green-green, which mean *good night* and *sleep well*. Through the binoculars, Frederik saw Arim climbing back through the window and closing it behind him, switching the light on in his room and a moment later drawing the curtains across. Frederik did the same with his curtains and sat for a moment looking at the Vampirella comic with its horrible story of the woman who ate rats. Down in the living room, his father was still singing away.

Ringo went down with Frederik when he joined the others. The negative was gone. Down in the living room, Frederik's mother said:

"My goodness, Frederik's come to keep us company!"

His father smiled, stopped singing and started tuning the guitar. Ringo hopped up to Anisette and again began to lick her neck until she started purring.

Margrethe was sitting on the floor by the fire with a mirror in front of her, trying to roll her hair around some pins. Their mother went out into the kitchen and returned with a tray of tea. She looked around the room and said:

"Aren't we nice and cozy?"

7

At the opposite end of Narum, in Hegn Road, Dan was sitting with his mother and father watching television. It was really his bedtime, but his father had said it would do him good to see this program, a program about Danish hospitals, and one of Dan's father's colleagues was taking part in it. The Minister of Health was in it, too, and in a round-table discussion at the end, his father's colleague and the Minister sat arguing and trying to remember to smile.

"That damned fool," said his father, about the Minister.

His mother looked up, but she had got used to his father swearing when Dan was in the room, especially when it concerned hospitals and the government. They were cutting down on money for hospitals, so that people had to lie and die in the corridors.

"But if we're to have new jet fighters, then you can be sure no one will cut down on *them*," said his father.

Dan knew his father got angry in this way. He grew excited when he was angry; but usually he seemed tired and grumpy in the evening.

The Minister of Health had the last word, and it was clear that the doctor whom Dan's father knew had not made his point. The chairman had sat looking at his watch all through the discussion.

"Bloody rubbish!" said his father, without getting up to switch off the television. "Sometimes," he went on, "I wonder whether *that* form of democracy is worth what we keep saying it is here in Denmark."

"Then you might well speak decently in your own home," said his mother.

31

She wasn't looking especially angry. The late television news began. The announcer looked as if even he thought the first news item he had was very important.

"It is possible that Mr. Kreiser, the American Secretary of State for Foreign Affairs, when he visits Denmark on Thursday, will have the opportunity while he is here to discuss the crisis situation in the Middle East with other people, as well as with the Danish Prime Minister," he said.

He looked down at his script and then up again.

"International news agencies imply this evening that Mr. Kreiser hopes to meet representatives of the Arab countries as well as the Palestine Liberation Army in Denmark before going on to Moscow."

A picture of Kreiser came on the screen.

"Mr. Kreiser refused to confirm this statement this evening. It was confirmed that he would be a guest at lunch on Thursday at Fredensborg Palace, at which Her Majesty the Queen and Prince Henrik would be hosts."

A picture of Fredensborg Palace came on the screen.

"At a press conference this afternoon, it was announced that the police are taking more comprehensive security measures than have ever been used before in connection with a foreign state visit. Over three thousand policemen were expected to be on duty for the motorcade as it drives from Kastrup Airport to Fredensborg."

The Queen and Prince Henrik appeared on the screen.

"Members of the Home Guard are also expected to be posted along the route, and police forces on duty are expected to be heavily armed to protect Kreiser and his entourage from any attempt at assassination."

The announcer drew a deep breath.

"Today there was again a serious decline in both shares and dividends on Copenhagen's stock exchange."

Dan's father got up and switched the television off.

"Yes," he said. "They can find the money for *that*. Police and Home Guards and a lavish lunch at the palace. But people who are lying dying in hospital corridors. . . ."

"Fredensborg Palace?" Dan interrupted him. "Then they'll be coming along the motorway, won't they?"

"Ye-es," said his father.

"So they'll be going through Narum?" said Dan.

His father nodded, looking tired.

Dan wondered if, with all those police and Home Guard posted around, people would be allowed to stand on the bridge over the motorway, where they could catch a glimpse of the motorcade and Kreiser's car, which was bound to be something out of the ordinary, presumably bullet-proof.

Dan's mother told him to go to bed. The last thing Dan thought about before he fell asleep was that he was standing on the bridge over the motorway and Kreiser's car was passsing underneath the bridge. Dan had his heavy schoolbag on the outside of the railing and could hit the car windshield with the bag, if he aimed correctly, and if the police and the Home Guard hadn't already discovered what he was up to and arrested or shot him.

TUESDAY

8

Dan cycled to school. It was a cold morning and it looked like snow. It had been a mild winter, and Dan reckoned that if it began to snow, there was a good chance they would get the day off from school.

Just before the shopping center, he saw a police car, which had pulled in to the side. There was no one in it, so they were probably out checking the crossroads before the bridge. Dan switched his light on. It was such heavy going that it reminded him of his father's exercising bicycle down in the basement at home.

But there was no one directing the traffic at the crossroads, and when Dan had crossed over, he switched off his light again. Up on the motorway bridge, he saw two men in light-colored raincoats. One of them had something in his hand which he seemed to be protecting with his raincoat. Dan put a spurt on. It was a long time since he had seen two men in uniforms and white raincoats like those.

The black thing the man was trying to hide seemed to be a transistor radio, but when Dan had put his bike down and begun to walk toward the two men, he saw that it was a walkie-talkie with antennae, microphone and the lot. The man had just lifted it to his mouth and he was so occupied with fixing it and at the same time arguing with the other man that Dan was able to get right up behind him without being noticed and listen to what was being said.

The two men couldn't get the walkie-talkie to work, and they were arguing about what was wrong with it. "Let me try," said the man who didn't have the walkie-talkie, and when the other man refused to let it go, it sounded as if they were about to quarrel seriously.

The first policeman—for they must be policemen—finally got the apparatus to say something, and it hummed and crackled. Dan was now very close to them, pretending to be hunting for something in his schoolbag. He also glanced at his watch; for once he had got away in good time. There were twelve minutes to go before he had to be in school.

"Hello," said the policeman into the microphone, just behind Dan's back, "we're in position forty-six. Hello, forty-five, can you hear me?"

They obviously couldn't, because not a sound came out of the walkie-talkie.

"You should say 'Roger and over,' " said the other policeman. "And then you press that button there."

"Roger and over," said the first policeman.

"No, no," snarled the other man. "Not *that* button, the other one. Look now, there, you see?"

"Roger and over," repeated the first policeman.

"Yes, we can hear you perfectly well," came out of the walkie-talkie. "And what's more we can see you, too. How do you keep your raincoats so clean? Roger and over."

"Okay," said the policeman. "And no funny talk, if you don't mind. So we have both visual and . . . and . . ."

"Audio," whispered the other man.

"Visual and audio contact. We can also see you. And we have driven through the stretch between position forty-four and position forty-six with our patrol car under stimulated emergency circumstances. . . ."

"*Sim*ulated emergency circumstances," whispered the other man.

"Yes, simulated, and we have timed it at nearly six minutes, including a rapid sprint from parked patrol vehicle to position. We calculate that we can save a minute, if we can park the car direct on the position. Over and Roger. Sorry, Roger and over."

The two policemen came back and started arguing about how they were to switch over from sender to receiver, and Dan looked around for the other walkie-talkie. He gazed down toward the next bridge and saw two men who had taken up position there.

At last they got through and a voice in the walkie-talkie began to speak.

"Okay, come on, you must have found out how that toy works by now. Six minutes, we make it. Have you contact with position forty-seven?"

Dan looked in the other direction, northward toward the next bridge, and the two men beside him turned simultaneously. They were clearly surprised to find someone standing behind them.

"No," replied the policeman standing beside Dan. "But I expect you've had difficulty checking with position forty-eight."

The man without a walkie-talkie whispered eagerly to the other man.

"We must find out if there's any need for between-stations between us and forty-five."

"Yes," said policeman number one into his microphone. "Is there any need for between-positions between us and you? Is there a road or a parking place or something like that up to the motorway between our main positions? Over and . . . sorry, Roger and over."

"Yes," replied the voice in the receiver, "there's the camping site. The access road to the camping site is to be blocked on Thursday morning, where the streetcar cuts across it."

"How long before countdown?" asked the policeman beside

Dan, at the same time beginning to look with annoyance at Dan.

"A little less of that space stuff, if you don't mind," said the voice in the receiver. "As early in the morning as we can get there."

The policeman with the walkie-talkie turned sharply to Dan. "What are *you* doing here?"

"Hello," said the receiver. "What's that?"

"Push off, will you," said the policeman. "This is nothing to do with you."

"You're cops, aren't you?" said Dan.

"No," said the man, going red in the face.

"Scram, and fast," said the other policeman.

"What are you doing?" said Dan. "Is it something to do with Kreiser?"

"Who the hell are you standing there talking to?" came the receiver.

"You're ensuring that no one shoots Kreiser on Thursday, aren't you?" said Dan. "You're practicing, aren't you?"

"No," said the policeman, without conviction.

"Huh," said the receiver. "You've attracted some spies already, have you? If only you would wear *gray* raincoats."

The man without a walkie-talkie went up to Dan and gave him a shove.

"Scram," he said, as Dan tried to keep his balance.

Dan looked at his watch. It was six minutes to eight and he would have to hurry if he wasn't going to be late.

"Search him immediately," said the voice in the receiver. "It might be an enemy agent disguised as a boy on his way to school!"

The person in the receiver began to laugh.

The policeman who had given Dan a shove went up to him and looked as if he were about to do so again. Dan turned around and calmly walked back to his bike.

A moment later, he passed the two policemen in civilian

clothes. They had now turned toward the next motorway bridge, and once again seemed to be having trouble getting the walkie-talkie to work.

9

In their social-studies lesson, Mr. Jensen announced that they would have a discussion about the situation in the Middle East.

Discussion, thought Dan. That always meant that the teacher talked for ninety-nine percent of the time.

Dan was sitting in the middle of the row, between his two best friends, Frederik and Arim.

"Those of you who saw the television news yesterday or have read the papers lately will know that another war may be brewing up in the Middle East," said Mr. Jensen. "If anything comes of it, it'll be the fifth. But can any of you explain *why* there'll be war in the Middle East?"

No one put a hand up or said anything, and neither did Mr. Jensen look as if he expected anyone to.

"As the Israelis and the Arabs both say themselves, what they are fighting about is the Palestinian problem," he went on. "The fact is, a lot of people used to live in what we now call Israel, and which was then called Palestine, just after the Second World War. With the United Nations' blessing, Palestine was given to the Jews, who created the new state of Israel and drove the Palestinian population out."

Mr. Jensen got up and appeared to be looking in his pocket for his cigarettes.

"The Europeans had a guilty conscience about the Jews," he said. "Hitler had put them into concentration camps and murdered millions of them. Not that it can really be said that other

Europeans treated the Jews especially well, either. Then, to make amends, they were to be given back their old country, and now the Palestinians had to get out. *But....*"

Mr. Jensen had obviously given up trying to find what he was looking for in his pockets.

"But is it only the Palestinians all these wars are about? No, it isn't. The fact is that the rich countries have pumped money into Israel ever since the Second World War. So now it's there and is a rich country right in the middle of the Arab world, which until recently has been poor, because in the past we bought the only thing they have to offer at too low a price. Oil, of course. The wars in the Middle East have not, therefore, been old-fashioned wars between two peoples. They have been wars between the rich people and the poor. And neither have they been wars between different races. For both Jews and Arabs are Semites. So the Arabs are not being anti-Semitic when they . . . Yes?"

Dan had put up his hand. The way Mr. Jensen was talking you could tell that he favored the Arabs and was against Israel. He had said several times that they should interrupt if they had something sensible to say. Dan thought he had.

"Yes?" said Mr. Jensen. "Dan? Do you want to ask something?"

"Yes," said Dan. "I want to ask if you're a Communist."

Mr. Jensen stood thinking for a moment. Then he again began to hunt for whatever it was he had in his pocket and at last found it—a packet of cigarettes and a lighter. He calmly lighted a cigarette before answering.

"Dan, you know perfectly well the ballot is secret in Denmark, don't you?"

"Yes, but . . ."

"So, I needn't answer your question, need I? But all the same, I'm glad you asked it. You see I'm trying to tell you things as I think they are. With equal weight on how both parties see them. But . . .''

He inhaled deeply and blew out a smoke ring.

"But one *can't* do that. And so it is probably better that one admits one's viewpoint and says how one stands oneself, and what one thinks oneself, isn't it? Then later on, one can try to be fair toward all parties, without having guaranteed that one is, can't one?''

"Yes,'' said Dan. "But . . .''

"Yes," said Mr. Jensen. "I did in fact vote for the Communists at the last election. And I am for the poor countries against the rich ones, because the war they are waging is another form of class struggle. I don't have to be a Communist to think that. But I am. Stop sitting there laughing, please.''

He had said that because there was a lot of amusement at Dan getting Mr. Jensen to say how he had voted, and perhaps also because their teacher was standing there smoking in the middle of a lesson.

Dan thought it was great of him to say how he had voted, so that you knew where you had him. Dan had no idea how any of the other teachers voted; their music teacher, for instance, who was teaching them new patriotic songs, and who played the piano much too loudly.

Mr. Jensen got them to quiet down. He told them about living standards in the Arab countries and Israel, and how the four wars had gone, and about how the Palestinians were now stuck in camps, but that that was also the fault of the Arabs.

"Yes, Dan?'' he said, when Dan put his hand up a second time.

"You said we could ask what we liked, didn't you?'' he said.

"Yes. What is it now?''

"How much do you earn per year?''

The class laughed loudly at Dan's question, but Mr. Jensen

did not, and when he had quietened them down again and lighted another cigarette from the stub of the first one, he said:

"You mean you can't be a Communist and earn as much as I do?"

"I just want to know," said Dan.

"That's all right," said Mr. Jensen. "I earn about a hundred thousand kroner. But that's the money I earn, not a bribe. It is not a bribe to stop thinking what I think. Are you satisfied with that answer?"

"Yes," said Dan, who was thinking he had been cheeky enough. He wouldn't have liked it if Mr. Jensen had started an investigation into who in the class got the most pocket money.

Mr. Jensen went on talking, but now there were others who had plucked up the courage to ask personal questions. One wanted to know how much his wife earned, and that, he said, had nothing whatsoever to do with anyone in the class. Another wanted to know how much he gave in aid for underdeveloped countries, and received the reply that he paid about a thousand kroner into different organizations, but that he would prefer to pay what should be paid through his taxes.

When it was quiet again, Mr. Jensen started telling them about the PLO, the Palestinian Liberation Organization, which was behind the hijackings and what people called terrorist activities.

"It is not pleasant," he said. "But perhaps it is the only thing they can do to get reasonable treatment. You have to understand that these people are idealists and they do not do these things for money. They risk their lives for a cause they believe in."

It was Frederik who put his hand up this time. Mr. Jensen was looking rather tired.

"Yes, Frederik?"

"I think you're beating about the bush," said Frederik. "I don't think you've really said whether you agree with these terrorist things and innocent hostages and all that. *Do* you?''

Frederik was asking the question quite seriously; he was not being "cheeky," and both the class and Mr. Jensen realized this.

"You know, Frederik," he said finally. "I just don't know. Neither do I know if there is anyone any longer that one can call innocent.''

"Children, for instance," said Arim.

"Yes... well," said Mr. Jensen. "No," he went on suddenly. "No, hell no, I don't agree with them. I can't bear them. I can understand them, but I'm against such actions, full stop.''

After he had said that, Mr. Jensen looked relieved. Dan also thought better of him than he had when the lesson had begun.

Mr. Jensen spent the rest of the lesson telling them about Henry Kreiser, himself a Jew, but who had hurtled around the Middle East in a jet so much that in the end the Arabs had probably more confidence in him than the Israelis had.

"My opinion is—and I *am* a Communist—is that he has a lot of murky things on his conscience—among others, Vietnam and Cambodia. But there is a chance that he can also do something sensible in between. So I thought . . .''

He smiled.

" . . .we would go out to say hello to him as he whizzes through Narum on Thursday. We could take the opportunity to study Danish security operations,'' he added.

The bell rang.

"And you can bring your little Danish flags with you, so far as I'm concerned,'' he said. "But preferably no bouquets, for the police are heavily armed and nervous, and they might think there were hand grenades or stink bombs in the flowers.''

During recess, Dan went with Arim and Frederik down into the boys' lavatories and they shared a cigarette, but not one of them could blow a smoke ring as well as Mr. Jensen.

10

After school, Arim and Dan cycled over to the swimming pool to settle a bet over who could swim two hundred meters the fastest. Frederik came after he had taken his sister home.

It had grown much colder, but it hadn't snowed yet. There were now two police motorcycles parked just before the motorway bridge, but they saw no one who looked like a policeman. Dan told the other two about what had happened that morning.

The swimming pool was more crowded than they had expected, mostly with little kids splashing around in the shallow end of the pool, or who were swimming about across the lanes. Nevertheless, Arim, Dan, and Frederik tried to settle their bet, and they began to bump into the little kids who wouldn't budge, although they shouted at them to get out of the way. An attendant called them over to the edge of the pool and told them that either they were to swim quietly or else get out.

They decided to settle the bet another day, which suited Arim very well, because he had noticed at once that he was a bit slower than the other two. He immediately decided he would go to the pool a few times on his own to get into better form before they tried again.

Shortly afterward, Dan and Frederik said they were going home to exchange comics; but Arim stayed, in the hopes that the crowd would thin out and he could train a bit. But it didn't, on the contrary, so finally Arim practiced diving once or twice and then went into the sauna.

It was full up in there and a fat man, who looked as if he were about to perspire to death, told Arim that it was a sauna for adults.

"I *am* fourteen," said Arim.

"That you're not?" said the fat man, laughing.

The others laughed too, and it seemed as if they would gladly have let Arim stay, but Arim felt that it shouldn't be like that.

He went and got dressed, got on his bike and set off. If he couldn't get fit that way, he thought, he would try another. On his way toward Trorod, he managed to overtake several mopeds and by the time he got up over the motorway in Old Holte, he was out of breath and felt good.

He stopped on the bridge to get his breath back. It was getting dark now, but there was no sign of the police there, so he didn't bother to switch on his light. He rode homeward over on the other side of the motorway along the crooked little road which they had made to a new building.

In front of him in the gray light, he saw two red rear lights. A large moving van had pulled in to the side and two men were standing kicking at one of the rear wheels. It was obviously punctured, and Arim thought he would like to see how you changed a wheel on such a large truck. He wasn't so interested in cars as Dan was, but he was still out of breath and could do with a bit of rest.

The men had noticed him. They were talking together and Arim realized that they weren't speaking Danish. On the back of the moving van, the word "Denmark" was painted in large letters. The men were speaking English, and when he got nearer, he realized that they were the same two men who had been buying a doll in the toy store the day before.

How strange, he thought. English foreign workers in a Danish furniture-moving company? The men spotted him and this appeared to be the reason why they stopped talking.

A car approached from behind, passed Arim and the moving van, but then parked off the road. It was a taxi with its meter light on, to show it was free. Well, thought Arim, perhaps

44

they'll get some help changing the wheel now, or perhaps they've run out of gas.

There were two men in the taxi, one of whom got out, the other remaining at the wheel. Now there were three men standing there speaking English. Arim cycled slowly toward them and at first they lowered their voices, then ceased talking altogether. He would have liked to have chatted with the two Englishmen again, but they didn't appear to recognize him. Neither did they appear to want to talk to him, so he cycled slowly on.

The taxi was a Mercedes. Arim didn't know much about makes of cars, but of course he recognized the star on the radiator. He heard the three men beginning to speak English again, and when he was a bit farther on and turned around, he saw that the fourth man had got out of the taxi, having switched off the engine as well as the lights.

Arim had got his breath back again now and rode home as fast as he could. It was a "Danish" day at home today, and his father had promised that not only would they have pork and peas, but that he would also bake an apple cake which would be "more Danish than the Danes can make themselves." Whatever he meant by that.

Dan and Frederik were exchanging comics at Dan's place. When they'd done so, Frederik remembered something and said:

"Dan, do you know how you take photographs with those Polaroid films?"

"No," said Dan. "You'll have to ask Arim that. His father's a photographer."

"Yes," said Frederik. "I would have asked him, but I forgot. I meant to tell him that he must get on and learn the Morse code, too."

Frederik was putting the comics into his bag.

"You don't know much about cars, do you?" Dan said to him.

Frederik shook his head.

"Why?" said Dan. "Why would a taxi driver be driving around with a six-cylinder gasoline engine saying that it's a diesel engine? And what's more, why was there a diesel sign on the back of the car?"

"To fool the enemy," said Frederik, closing his bag.

Dan grinned, but when Frederik had gone, he couldn't get the words out of his head.

To fool the enemy.

Frederik rode home. There were still two police motorbikes standing just before the motorway bridge. He must be a big bug, this Henry Kreiser, thought Frederik, spinning on down the empty road along which the streetcar ran, and then on home to the house in the forest. The warning light was already blinking, but he got over in good time. Then he realized that the road through the wood was darker than usual.

The road lamps were out and he wondered if the lights were off at home, too. Fortunately, they weren't, and he was pleased when he saw the lighted windows of his own house.

11

"Aren't we nice and cozy?" said Frederik's mother.

"Yes," said Frederik's father, "but I don't like it when the telephone is out of order."

The fire had been lighted and Ringo was in the basket with Anisette, licking her between the ears. Margrethe had borrowed a skirt from her mother and was busy turning it up, as it was far too long. Frederik was thinking about the fact that he had two new comics up in his room, one a Hitchcock, the other the latest number of Giggler.

"Isn't the phone working?" said his mother. "It was all right this afternoon when I spoke to Otto."

"I expect Dad's worn it out," said Frederik. Otto and Frederik's father often went shooting together, and Otto's hunting stories were endless.

"No," said his father. "But it's not working now. I wanted to phone Rasmussen and discuss where we shall be going tomorrow. Frederik, would you bike up to the station and find out if it's the exchange that's out of order, or just *our* phone?"

Frederik said he would and it was not until he was on his way from the house that he remembered that there were no lights on the road to the streetcar. Well, he wasn't afraid of riding in the dark.

It was frosty out now, and he rode fast to keep warm. When he was halfway through the wood, he saw a light in front of him, a vehicle heading toward him, and he could hear that it was something like a truck. Rasmussen, probably, who had come in the truck because he hadn't been able to contact Dad. Frederik rode up on the footpath so as not to block the narrow road.

But it wasn't Rasmussen. As the truck came nearer, Frederik saw that it was enormous. He moved back in between the trees to let it pass. It wasn't going especially fast and it only had its sidelights on. It was a moving van, he realized as it passed him. It appeared to be red and on the side of it "Denmark" was painted in large letters.

The truck disappeared behind Frederik and he remained standing in the dark for a moment, thinking. A moving van on its way to the forest ranger's house at this time of night? Could it be that someone thought the camping site was open in the winter?

Where the road ran into the forest there were two signs which

47

said clearly "Road closed. No admittance to unauthorized persons" on one of them, and "Camping site closed" on the other. Both notices were put up each winter.

Funny.

Frederik cycled across the streetcar tracks. The lights were on here, and he cycled up to the station and went in to ask at the ticket office whether their telephone was working. Yes, it was, the woman said, lifting the receiver so that he could hear for himself. He went into the telephone booth and was just about to dial the number his father had told him to ring to report their phone out of order, when he discovered he had only one twenty-five-ore coin. He went out and asked the woman if he could borrow twenty-five ore from her. She was speaking on the phone.

It was a very long conversation, even longer than the kind his father had with Otto. No one came and interrupted the woman to buy tickets. After Frederik had stood there for a while, he knocked on the glass. The woman looked up at him and shook her head before going on talking.

After Frederik had stood there a while longer, waiting for her to finish her conversation, he began to get cold. It would soon be nine o'clock, and Arim would shortly be on his balcony with his flashlight. Suddenly Frederik couldn't be bothered to wait there freezing any longer. When he got home perhaps the telephone would be working again. If not, perhaps he'd have to tell a fib and say he'd reported the fault. Then he could cycle to the station later, if the telephone was still out of order in the evening.

He had quite forgotten the moving van, but he remembered it as he rode back, because he saw the deep tracks, as if it had been fantastically heavy. There was only one set of tracks as far as he could see, so it hadn't driven back again. The only place he could imagine it turning around would be in front of their house, as it couldn't possibly drive on through the forest.

As he approached the house, he realized that the lights above the front door and above the tall shed, where his father's tractor and car usually stood, were both out. What now? They were both usually on all night long. Had the electricity gone off, too? No, the lights were on indoors still.

In the light from the windows, Frederik saw that the big moving van with "Denmark" on it had stopped in front of the house. The lights and engine were switched off. What on earth was going on?

He put his bike aside and tried to open the door, but it was locked. He had put the bolt up when he left, but his mother must have been out and put it down again, as she thought it should always be locked at night. Frederik hauled out his key and stuck it into the keyhole, and the moment he did so, the door was opened from inside.

It was his father who opened the door, and he opened it only very slightly. Frederik had never seen his father look so peculiar. He was very pale, except for a large red patch on each cheek.

"Frederik," he said.

"Yes," said Frederik.

"Listen, now," said his father, gulping visibly. "Something's happened, but there's no need at all to be afraid. Just come on inside quietly, will you?"

"Yes," said Frederik. "What's happened?"

"Just come on in quietly," said his father, opening the door just wide enough for Frederik to slip inside.

In the hall, apart from his father, were his mother and sister. Behind them, slightly hidden by the door, were three strange men. And two steps up the stairs to the first floor was a fourth man with a revolver in his hand. He was pointing it straight at Frederik.

49

12

"Good evening, Frederik," said the man with the revolver.
"Hurry up inside, will you, so that we can close the door."

"Just do what the man says," said his father.

Frederik went in and his father closed the door behind him.
Was this a joke, or what was it all about? Something told
Frederik that it was no joke. His mother was standing clutching
Margrethe to her. Margrethe was still wearing the much-too-
long skirt.

"Frederik," said the man with the revolver. "There are four
of us here and we have come to live in your house for a while. I
will explain a little more in a moment. But first of all you must
tell me if you managed to get through to the telephone exchange."

Frederik thought for a moment. What if he lied and said yes?
The man on the stairs was fair, his hair short. He was wearing
steel-rimmed glasses and had bright-blue eyes. Two of the other
men had long dark hair and dark skins. They did not look
Danish. The fourth was the most horrible, because he had a
black mask over the top part of his face. Frederik noticed that all
four men were wearing thin gloves.

"Tell them the truth," said his father.

"I hadn't enough money," said Frederik. "And I couldn't
borrow the woman's telephone, so . . ."

"Good, Frederik," said the man on the stairs, in a voice
which in fact sounded soft and friendly. "I hope we can trust
you. You see, if you're lying or doing anything silly like that,
then you are risking lives. Perhaps all our lives, but anyhow your
little sister's. So you didn't get through?"

"No," said Frederik.

The man hidden behind the half-mask said in a low voice:
"A hell of an amateurish start. We *must've* passed the kid."
The man on the stairs said:
"Good. The telephone will be in order in half an hour, if no one does anything foolish. And that's true of everything on the whole: it'll work *only* if no one does anything foolish. It's true of . . ."
He looked at the other three men.
"That's true of us, too," he said. "And now we've a lot to do in the next hour. First and foremost we must get the truck under cover. When that's done, we can fix the lights out on the road again. And then the telephone, in that order."
He looked at the man in the mask.
"You take the kids upstairs and look around carefully. You"
—he looked at one of the two other men—"stay with Mrs. Poulsen and go through these rooms. You"—meaning the other dark-haired man—"and I'll go out with Poulsen and get the truck into place. Watch out for the animals—the dog, anyhow."
The man in the mask set about translating into English. What he had said in Danish had been with a slight accent. He didn't speak English especially quickly, so Frederik understood most of it. After he had translated, he calmly took Frederik by the hand and went over to Mrs. Poulsen. Margrethe began to cry, but her mother remained calm.
"Go with Frederik and the man," she said, "and nothing will happen. This is rather horrible, but these strangers won't do anything to us if we do what they say."
While his mother was comforting Margrethe, Frederik was trying to think. At first he had been so surprised that he had been quite unable to think. But now it was all too horribly clear. They had been taken as hostages, all four of them. And it appeared that these men were going to stay in the house. Why? Frederik thought about the faded negative which he'd found on

the slope down toward the motorway. Then he thought about Henry Kreiser.

He had read in a newspaper that most hostages were released. Someone had calculated that more than half were. Frederik discovered that his legs had begun to tremble beneath him and he envied Margrethe, who probably didn't understand much of it all, and who was fortunate enough to be able to do nothing but cry.

His mother had persuaded Margrethe to go with the stranger, and it helped when Frederik was allowed to drop the stranger's hand and hold his own out to Margrethe.

"Look," said his mother to Margrethe, in a voice that was close to breaking. "Look—the man's got a funny mask on. Perhaps he's going to the carnival, like you."

Margrethe isn't that small or stupid, thought Frederik. And indeed, Margrethe was not consoled, but cried even more. Halfway upstairs, it became too much for the man in the mask and he placed his hand over her mouth, nervously glancing at Frederik.

The man who had given orders in Danish went outside with Frederik's father and one of the dark-haired men. The other man went with Frederik's mother into the living room. It all seemed to be quite peaceful in a way, except for the sound of Margrethe weeping.

The man had thrust his free hand into the pocket of the thin black jacket he was wearing on top of a track suit. The pocket bulged and Frederik had little doubt about what was in it.

At first they were both shooed into Margrethe's room, where they were ordered over by the window and the man kept glancing at them as he searched through Margrethe's closet and bed. He heaved a whole lot of toys onto the floor and appeared not to know what it was he was looking for. Then he drew the curtains across and ordered them into Frederik's room.

Here he did the same thing. But this time, he found something he could confiscate: Frederik's transistor radio and binoculars, which had been lying on the windowsill. He also took Frederik's flashlight out of the closet, but put it back again with a heap of horror comics. He opened the window and stood for a moment looking down toward the motorway. Then he closed it again, drew the curtains and, with Frederik and Margrethe ahead of him, went into the bathroom.

There he drew the curtains, too, and took a packet of razor blades and two pairs of nail scissors out of the cabinet. Then he ordered Frederik and Margrethe into their parents' bedroom.

He spent a long time in there, drawing the curtains, pulling the telephone plug out of the wall and taking the telephone with him, searching through drawers, finding a pocket knife in one of Dad's jackets, a paperknife on Mother's bedside table. Out on the landing, he stopped for a moment, then he pushed Margrethe into her room, told her to lie down on her bed and not move, then turned to Frederik.

In good Danish, he said to Frederik:

"And no accidents, please. Come with me, now, and if you get up to any little tricks, then I'll get up to a big one. Got me?"

Frederik nodded. The door into the living room was ajar and he caught a glimpse of his mother and one of the dark-haired men rummaging through the chest-of-drawers. The dark-haired man was standing with their old box camera in his hand, saying:

"Camera?"

Frederik's mother nodded and the man shook his head and slipped the camera in with the things that were to be taken away.

"No cameras," he said. "No photos here."

The man in the mask pushed Frederik out through the front door into the yard.

"If you get up to any little tricks," he repeated, "I'll get up to a big one."

13

Out in the yard, Frederik watched the fair-haired Dane directing his father as he drove a tractor to the front of the house. The tractor normally stood in the garage, which was deep enough to hold two tractors as well as their car. It was really a kind of barn which they used as a garage. His father had already driven the car out.

When both the car and the tractor were parked alongside the barn, the Dane went and got into the driver's seat of the moving van. Frederik couldn't help being impressed. The barn door was just high and wide enough to allow the moving van inside. They must have come here one night and measured the barn door, he thought. Perhaps they had taken photographs of it with that Polaroid film.

Professional—that's what they were. Did that give them all a better chance of survival now? Or, to the contrary, less chance? There was something wrong with Frederik's legs; his knees felt like water and he couldn't control his legs.

The garage door was closed behind the moving van, and they all went back into the house. Frederik's father gave his shoulder a quick squeeze before the fair-haired man ensured that they were kept well apart from each other.

"Get the kid down again," said the Dane to the man in the mask.

A short while later, the Poulsen family and their four uninvited guests were sitting in the living room. The fire was roaring in the fireplace, Ringo howling faintly out in the kitchen, and Anisette meowing offendedly in the pantry.

Margrethe was crying again, although she had been allowed

to sit by her mother, and the fair man turned to the man in the mask.

"The doll," he said.

The man vanished and returned with a large doll, which he handed to Margrethe. Slowly the doll closed its eyes as it fell out of Margrethe's hands backward onto the sofa.

The Dane had gone over to the telephone and lifted the receiver; the dialing tone had come back again.

"That's that," he said. "The phone's working again. But we've taken away the phone upstairs, should anyone feel like using it. Down here the phone can be answered by you, Mrs. Poulsen, or you, Mr. Poulsen, if anyone rings. And someone probably will."

The Dane was disturbed by a slight sound. It was Margrethe, who had picked up the doll so that it said *ma-ma*. Frederik understood why the man was so scared, because the sound was both very real but at the same time quite false.

"It goes without saying that we'll be listening to what is said. But we can't run the risk of anyone thinking it's peculiar that the telephone doesn't ring or that no one answers. From now on, it is a question of no one noticing anything. And that no one wants to come and see you."

"For how long?" asked Frederick's father.

"Okay," said the Dane. "You want an answer. Thirty-six hours, if all goes well. Poulsen, you must ring early tomorrow morning to your colleagues and say you've got illness in the house. And tell the men to get on working on their own. If your orders are misunderstood or anything, then you know whose life goes first. And Mrs. Poulsen . . ."

Frederik's mother looked up and Frederik couldn't help thinking: this should have been a cozy evening.

"Yes," she said, just as calmly as her husband.

"If they phone from the school, then the children are ill."

"What's inside the moving van?" asked Frederik's father.

"More toys," said the man in the mask.

"It's Kreiser you're after, isn't it?" said Frederik's father.

"Yes," replied the Dane. "It's him—or us. And by *us* I always mean it's your little girl who will die first, Mr. Poulsen."

The Dane took off his steel-rimmed spectacles and polished them swiftly before going on.

"You can believe me or not, but I loathe violence. I would very much like to drive away from here on Thursday without— without anyone having as much as a hair on his head hurt. I just don't think it'll be that easy. And what I'm going to do now will be *only* to save human lives. Not because I in any way care."

"Do now?" said Frederik's mother.

The man nodded and gave the others orders in English. They shut Ringo in the living room and ordered the Poulsen family to get up and go out into the yard. A cord the men had brought with them was put through Ringo's collar and out in the yard the man in the mask let Ringo go. He ran confusedly as far as the cord allowed him. He ran toward Frederik and stood whining on the tight cord.

The fair-haired Dane fixed something onto the barrel of his revolver. Frederik had seen enough films to know that it was a silencer. He realized what was going to happen and suddenly noticed that his legs, which had been feeling weak for a long time, were beginning to shake. At the same time everything began to float before his eyes. He wanted to do something to help Ringo, but he also wanted to bend down to get the blood to run back to his head.

The Dane raised the revolver and aimed it at Ringo. He stood for a long time taking aim. Then he lowered the revolver again.

"Hell, no," he said. "That's too feeble. Shooting a dog to show that you're prepared to shoot people."

"We *did* understand that," said Frederik's father.

"God knows if you did," said the Dane. "God knows if anyone understands this without having tried it. If I'd been logical, then I'd have shot your daughter at once and had your son prepared as the next on the list. You see, I *have* already killed people, haven't I? And I'll kill many more in the next two days."

"Will you?" said Frederik's father. "Many more?"

"Yes, I will. So it's fatuous to spare a dog."

The Dane went up to Ringo and took off the collar with his name and address on it and gave him a new collar. As far as Frederik could see, it was a choker collar, and then the Dane gave orders that Ringo was to be locked into the basement and not let out at any time.

But Frederik wasn't taking in all that much, because everything was now swimming in front of his eyes. Suddenly he crouched down, unable to keep his balance, a violent thumping in his temples, and the last thing he remembered was two gloved hands grabbing him from behind so that he should not fall over backward.

When Frederik came to, he was lying in Margrethe's room. A camp bed had been placed alongside Margrethe's and the man in the mask was bending over him, handing him a glass of fruit juice. When Frederik opened his mouth, two pills were swiftly pushed into it, and he was forced to swallow them.

"They're only sleeping tablets," said the man. "We thought you deserved to sleep well after the tough evening you've had. And we could do with a bit of rest ourselves, too."

The man locked the door from the outside. Frederik thought sleepily that perhaps he could climb out of the window, but he realized that would cost Margrethe her life. The fair-haired Dane had said that he had already killed a lot of people. And that he reckoned on having to kill several more soon.

Frederik thought that his life had been quite changed and that never again would it be the same. Then he was overwhelmed by an enormous yawn and a moment later he noticed that he was about to fall asleep although he definitely didn't want to.

14

Arim was standing on the balcony wondering what on earth was going on. It was a quarter past nine and only four hours ago he'd said good-bye to Frederik and agreed that they would signal again this evening. Now it was a quarter of an hour past the time. Frederik must have forgotten. But that wasn't like Frederik. It was the first time he hadn't kept to an agreement to signal since they had been given the flashlights.

Arim tried one last time to signal the green-green-green which meant that their conversation could start, but there was no reply, so he realized it was hopeless.

The remarkable thing was that the lights had been on as usual over at the Poulsens' house when Arim had climbed out onto the balcony. Then the curtains had been drawn downstairs, at the same time as lights had gone on upstairs.

After that, something that Arim had never seen before had happened. Lights had gone on first in Frederik's room, then in the bathroom, and finally in the parents' bedroom. And not long after the lights had gone on, the curtains had been drawn.

Perhaps it hadn't been all that remarkable, but just that Arim had never seen it happen before. He knew the Poulsens and their habits from a great many visits to their house, and he knew what he could expect to see at about nine o'clock when he was standing waiting to signal.

Well, the only really remarkable thing now was that Frederik hadn't replied to Arim's signals. There had been a light on in Frederik's room, and the curtains had been drawn. Anyhow, Frederik couldn't say tomorrow that he hadn't been at home.

Arim had thought for a moment of phoning Frederik, but that would mean admitting that their signaling was more than a game. He might as well wait until tomorrow before complaining.

It was cold—freezing now—and a gust of wind caught the Christmas tree on the balcony and almost tipped it over. Arim glanced across at the Poulsens' house for one last time and saw that the lights on the road through the woods had been switched on. He had in fact not noticed that they had been out. Then he climbed quietly back through the window. He began to mend the yellow kite that had got smashed the day before.

WEDNESDAY

15

Arim and Dan met on the way to school. It was even colder than the evening before and the wind was just as strong. The two of them talked about whether they would get the day off for skiing if it snowed or whether they wouldn't if it didn't.

Where the road ran down toward the streetcar station, they stopped for a moment to wait for Frederik. But the minutes went by and he didn't come. Arim thought about Frederik's forgetting to signal the night before. Well, perhaps he'd been early this morning in exchange. But Frederik still hadn't come when the first lesson began. That's why, thought Arim. He's ill, and he was ill last night, too. Arim thought that you must be fairly seriously ill not to be able to get out of bed when alone in your room and signal as agreed.

Both Arim and Dan and most of the others were rather preoccupied in the first lesson. They had English and their English teacher was talking about the difference between English and American pronunciation. He was annoyed by the fact that more American than English was spoken on television. He was explaining that it was better to speak like Lord Peter Wimsey than like Kojak, whem Arim and Dan spotted the first snowflakes falling outside.

The snow was quite light, and they weren't given the day off at once. But during the course of the first recess, it snowed heavily and ten minutes after the second lesson had begun, the bell was rung for assembly and the school given a ski-day. The schoolyard was already covered with snow and it was crisp and cold; as it was below freezing, the snow crackled underfoot. Arim and Dan went home together again, agreed that they would go out skiing. It was tough on Frederik being ill and unable to come too, and they talked of phoning him and asking what was wrong. If Frederik was playing truant, he had certainly chosen the wrong day.

"We might as well . . ."

Arim was interrupted by a strange sound. They were standing by their bikes where the road went down to the streetcar station and Frederik's house. The air was thick with snow and they could hardly see up to the bridge over the motorway. Arim and Dan were both looking in the direction from which the noise was coming. Up in the swirling snow they could just see a black dot. It was quite a while before they realized what it was and why it was making such a row. It was a helicopter, and it was flying low in the direction of Copenhagen.

"Gosh," said Dan. "It can't find its way in the snow. That's why it's flying so low."

"Oh," said Arim, "they've got radar and all sorts of things. It can fly where it likes. If they were scared, they'd just fly higher up."

"Do you think so?" said Dan. He was usually the one who knew most about technical things, but Arim was probably right.

"Why the hell is it flying so low then?" said Dan.

"Because it's spying," said Arim. "I bet you it's one of the cops' helicopters. They're practicing for all that business tomorrow with Kreiser."

That might well be it—it fitted in. The helicopter flew on along the motorway in toward Copenhagen. Because of the snow, it was soon invisible again, as quickly as it had appeared, but they could still hear it buzzing a little.

"Well," said Dan. "Shall we run down and see what's up with Frederik?"

Arim nodded, and the two of them rode past the streetcar station and along the road to the Poulsens' house. They could see from the snow that no one else had been down there. Their hair and clothes were covered with snow, and they rode fast so as not to get cold, almost falling off once or twice because of the speed. In the yard between the Poulsen's house and the barn, they noticed that both the car and the tractor were outside. They went up and rang the front-door bell.

It was quite a long time before anything happened, and Dan had to ring again before he heard footsteps and Mrs. Poulsen appeared.

"G'morning," said Dan. "We've got the day off because of the snow, and so we came to see if Frederik was ill."

Mrs. Poulsen was usually very friendly, but she definitely wasn't today; in fact she was just about to close the door on them.

"What's wrong with Frederik?" Arim asked. "Is it infectious?"

"Yes," said Mrs. Poulsen, after hesitating for a moment. "It's infectious."

She was again just about to close the door when Dan asked:

"Is it measles?"

Mrs. Poulsen hesitated and looked as if she had to think before replying.

"Yes, it's measles. And both Margrethe and Frederik have got it. So you'd better . . ."

She was about to close the door properly this time.

" . . .go away quickly."

Dan took a step forward.

"I've had measles," he said. "So I can go up and say hello without it mattering."

"I've had measles, too," said Arim. He wasn't quite certain whether that was true, but he didn't want to be left standing alone in the snow.

"No," said Mrs. Poulsen. "That wouldn't be a good thing. We . . .we're not quite certain what it is. It could be . . ."

She stopped, and Dan and Arim both thought that it seemed as if she were just inventing things.

"It could be . . .German measles."

Dan couldn't really remember what that was, but there was something about getting German measles before you grew up. His father had told him that there were parents who deliberately let their children be infected with German measles, but he couldn't remember much about it now.

"Has the doctor been here?" he asked.

This time Mrs. Poulsen hesitated for so long that neither Dan nor Arim could make it out. She must know. Finally she said: "No."

"Have you sent for him?" asked Dan.

Mrs. Poulsen really seemed very peculiar now. It was a question you could only answer yes or no to, and yet she stood there thinking about it. She looked very pale and seemed nervous.

"No," she said finally. "Not yet," she said.

She was holding tightly onto the door, as if she suspected Dan and Arim of wanting to force their way into the house. And she was holding it only slightly ajar, as if she were afraid even more bacteria would come flying out if she opened it any wider.

"Now you two really must be off, so that you don't catch it," she said. "Good-bye, then."

Instead of waiting for Arim and Dan to say good-bye, she slammed the door shut. Neither of them had ever seen her so unfriendly before.

Dan and Arim cycled once around the yard before going back.

"If I was Mr. Poulsen, I'd put the tractor and the car in the garage in this weather," said Dan.

They cycled back through the woods and up onto the main road again.

"She seemed awfully peculiar," said Arim.

"Yes," said Dan. "Either you've got measles or you've got German measles, or else you've got something completely different. And then you send for the doctor, don't you?"

"Yes," said Arim. Dan's father was a doctor, after all, and he must know all about that.

On the motorway bridge, they stopped. It was good to see the cars driving quite slowly in the snow with their lights on, and they could hear that the helicopter had turned and was on its way back again.

"Don't you think it's just out checking on the traffic?" said Dan to Arim.

"No," said Arim. "I think it's practicing for tomorrow."

The helicopter came out of the snow clouds. It was painted blue and white and had "Police" on it.

"Wow, look how low it's flying," said Dan.

The helicopter flew over just above their heads, so that the snow swirled about more than ever, and then it continued northward along the motorway. Dan and Arim stood there for a while watching it. Finally Dan said:

"You, Arim. Where would *you* stand if you wanted to get that Kreiser guy?"

Arim thought for a moment before replying with a grin:

"I'd go down to the Poulsens' with my catapult."

Dan grinned too, and they both biked quickly home to get their skis out.

16

"Good morning, Frederik."

It was the Dane leaning over Frederik.

"You've slept like a log, no doubt," said the man. "You're not used to sleeping pills. And your sister's still fast asleep, I see."

Frederik couldn't remember ever sleeping so soundly before. He could usually remember something of what he'd dreamed, but he remembered nothing this time.

The man sat down on a chair by his bed. He looked about forty, and that wasn't just because of his short hair, which was blond, like his eyebrows. Behind the steel-rimmed spectacles, his eyes were bright blue and quite friendly. He had red cheeks and he appeared to have shaved very carefully that morning. He smelled of after-shave lotion. When Frederik looked at his hands, he noticed that they were shaking slightly. Otherwise the man was fantastically calm.

"Frederik," he said. "Look me straight in the eyes. Do you think you could do a bit of acting? If it was a matter of your sister's life—and your own? If it became necessary, do you think you could lie here and look as if you were ill?"

Frederik nodded uncertainly.

"Well," said the man. "We could give you a pill. But . . ."

Frederik saw that the man's hands were shaking quite a lot.

"But that's not so good, is it?" he went on. "If you take another sleeping pill, you'd just lie there talking nonsense, wouldn't you?"

Frederik didn't know what to say to that, so he said nothing. The man sat there looking more and more distant, and finally Frederik plucked up his courage and said:

"What's your name?"

"My name's Jorgen," the man replied.

"Why aren't you wearing a mask?" Frederik asked.

"I'd thought of leaving the country as soon as possible," said the fair-haired man, smiling. "And I wasn't thinking of coming back."

"But the other man, the one who speaks Danish, the one with an accent, he's got a mask."

"Yes," said the fair man. "That's his business."

"Is he Danish?"

"No."

"What's his name?"

"He didn't bother to tell us. But we call him Henry. Like a certain gentleman we're very interested in, all four of us. Henry or Henrik."

"Is he an Englishman?"

"What a lot of questions. Don't you see that he is incognito? You know, he doesn't even want *us* to know who he is or where he comes from."

"The two dark-haired ones," said Frederik. "Are they Arabs?"

"I don't think I'll tell you that either."

Frederik remembered Mr. Jensen saying that both the Arabs and the Israelis, the Jews, were *Semites*.

"Are they Semites?" he said.

The man smiled.

"Frederik," he said. "You ask too many questions. Now it's my turn to ask a question. Your mother says you've got a little camera. We didn't find it in your room. Where is it?"

"It's at the photographic store in the shopping center being fixed."

"Good," said the man. "You see, none of us particularly wants to be photographed."

The man looked distant again, listening for something. Frederik listened, too, and heard a strange noise coming closer. Suddenly the man ran over to the window and looked upward.

It was a helicopter, flying low over the house in the direction of Copenhagen. Frederik could hear that. The man did not return to Frederik's bed until the helicopter was out of earshot.

"They're keeping an eye on things," said the man. "But there's nothing to see here, is there?"

That was rather difficult to answer, but Frederik shook his head. The pills they'd given him made him feel very muzzy still.

"I should really have given you some tablets to make you sleep on. That's all right for your sister, as she's so young. But you're another matter. If I give you some more pills and someone comes, then you don't know what you're saying, and so we risk you lying there saying something silly. If I don't give you any pills, can we rely on you to say what we tell you to say?"

"Yes," said Frederik.

"Good. I was going to ask your mother to say you've got measles. But in that case you should have a high temperature if anyone we can't get rid of comes, shouldn't you? We'll just say that you've been kept at home so that you don't infect anyone else. That is, that you're being kept away from your sister, and that you can well get up. But the important thing is that you don't get up to any kind of tricks, isn't it?"

"Yes," said Frederik. When the man said nothing else, he asked: "What's inside the moving van?"

"Wouldn't you like to know?" said the man, grinning.

There was something about him that Frederik couldn't help liking. It was strange, when he knew that the man had already killed someone, and that he was thinking of killing several more people.

"How will you leave, when you . . ."

"When we've taken a shot or two at Henry Kreiser? Well, we have a plan," he said.

"You can't drive back the same way you've come," said

Frederik, regretting his words at once, because he had perhaps given the man a good idea.

"No, we can't do that, indeed," he said. "I think we're almost as bright as you are. What would you do?"

Frederik thought that he would drive on through the forest, but you couldn't do that in an ordinary car, so he would get hold of one of the forestry authority's jeeps. But he didn't say that. Then he would also have another car standing waiting somewhere, like bank robbers did on television.

"You don't want to help us, then?" said the man, laughing. "Well, then we'll have to find a way ourselves. Frederik," he went on. "You might as well get up and go down to your parents in the living room."

As Frederik got up, he saw the man take a pill out, half wake Margrethe and push the pill into her mouth. He opened a bottle of soda water he had with him and got her to swallow the pill.

The man locked the door to Margrethe's room behind him, and then he went with Frederik downstairs to the living room. Through the window on the stairs, Frederik saw that it was still snowing heavily and he wondered if that fitted in with the four men's plans.

17

"Isn't Frederik going with you?"

Dan and Arim were standing in the kitchen on Hegn Road. Dan's father had not yet gone to the hospital and had been helping Dan find his skis and wax them.

"No," said Dan. "Frederik's got measles."

"Has he?"

"Yes," said Arim. "Or German measles."

"Now, listen," said Dan's father. "Either he's got measles, or else he's got German measles. Where did you hear that?"

Dan and Arim told him that Frederik hadn't been to school, and that they'd been down to the Poulsens' house, and how Mrs. Poulsen had stood in the doorway and wouldn't let them in.

"Did she say if the doctor had been there?" asked Dan's father.

"She was funny," said Dan. "Perhaps she had measles herself. She seemed as if . . ."

"But had the doctor been there or hadn't he?"

"She said the doctor hadn't been there yet."

Dan's father stood there thinking for a moment.

"Of course, she'll have called a doctor," he said, mostly to himself. "And you two were with Frederik yesterday afternoon, weren't you?"

"Yes."

"Then perhaps we ought to know what's wrong with Frederik, too. Listen, you two. Go on over to Arim's now, will you? For his skis. Then wait for me over there. In the meantime, I'll ring Mrs. Poulsen and find out what's wrong over there. I could slip over myself and have a look at Frederik and Margrethe, whatever it is."

Dan went out onto the porch and put on his skis. Arim came with him, pushing his bike, while Dan tried out the surface. The wind had dropped and the snowflakes were larger now. On the way to Arim's they had a snowball fight with some kids they didn't know.

Arim's mother opened the door for them. His father wasn't at home. Arim and Dan got busy finding the skis, because if Dan's father found that Frederik had something serious, he might not even let them go out skiing.

But Arim couldn't find his skis anywhere. Finally his mother said:

"They're probably up in the attic. Go and see if they're in the studio."

Arim and Dan rushed up there and went into the studio, and while Arim was looking in the closets under the eaves, Dan looked around. He'd never been in the studio before. He pulled the cord so that the blind whipped up and then he could see right across the field and the motorway to the forest.

"Oh, what a super picture you could take from here."

Arim was still searching. On a table in front of Dan lay a camera with an enormous telescopic lens. Dan put it up to his eye and squinted out through it. He soon had the Poulsens' house in the sight. It was like looking through a fantastic pair of binoculars and you could clearly see the smoke coming out of the chimney. When Dan lowered the camera, he could just see someone in the Poulsens' living-room window. It wasn't Mrs. Poulsen, because she had been wearing light-colored clothes, and this person was wearing something dark, so it was probably Mr. Poulsen.

"Come and look," said Dan to Arim.

"Are you crazy?" said Arim. "You mustn't touch that camera, or Dad'll go wild if he finds out."

So Dan put the camera down. It was a question of getting away quickly now, and a moment later they had found Arim's skis and run down the stairs to the third floor.

Arim's mother was standing on the landing.

"Now, you two," she said. "Dan's father has phoned. Something about Frederik having measles. But they're not certain that it's measles. Dan's father wants to find out what it is and he's driving over to the Poulsens and will phone when he knows what it is. So you must stay here for the time being."

Arim and Dan sat down, disappointed. It would soon be twelve o'clock, and so more than half their free day had gone. It had stopped snowing, and when Arim looked at the thermometer outside the kitchen window, he saw that it was only one degree below freezing. Who knew how long the snow surface would hold.

Arim's mother made them some hot chocolate and then she went out, so they had the apartment to themselves. They sat looking at some comic books for a while without that many laughs. Then Dan said:

"What about just going?"

Arim shook his head.

"He'll phone in a moment, I expect."

"Can you answer the telephone up in the attic?"

"Yes," said Arim.

They bickered about it and in the end Dan said that if they couldn't even go up into the attic, then he was leaving. So Arim agreed, and they switched the telephone through and went on up.

Up in the attic, they lighted the fire in the tiled stove, read more comics and shared a cigarette which Arim's father had left in the ashtray just after he'd lighted it. When they'd finished it, Dan went and picked the camera up again. He placed himself over by the window and looked around again.

"Too bad we can only see Frederik's house from this side," he said. "We can't even see if Dad's car is there at the moment."

"Put that camera down," said Arim. "It's worth thousands of kroner."

Dan stood amusing himself by pretending he had dropped it, and then he put it down and went around looking at the pictures Arim's father had taken. Half of them were of Tunis and half of Denmark. One picture was of a woman with no clothes on and Arim had to push Dan to make him go on.

They sat down with their comics again.

"Why the hell doesn't the man phone?" said Dan.

71

18

"Do you feel like a bit of fresh air?" said the fair-haired man to Frederik.

Frederik shook his head. He felt more like going into the living-room to see how things were with his parents. He also wanted to go down into the basement to see how Ringo was. And Anisette, for that matter.

"Well," said the man, "you'll have to come with me, anyhow."

Frederik realized that the man wanted him as a hostage, and there was nothing he could do about it. The door into the yard was opened, the man looked around once, then pushed Frederik out ahead of him.

When Frederik was standing out in the snow, he thought of something he would have thought of long before if he hadn't felt so thick in the head. It was snowing, so they had probably been given the day off at school. And when they had the day off . . .

His thoughts were interrupted because he had caught sight of something. The double doors of the barn were still closed, but the little loft window was open, and out of the window was thrust the barrel of what was clearly a machine gun.

Very clever, he thought. The machine gun was directed straight at the road up from the woods, the only way cars could approach. But what would happen if anyone came on foot from the other direction?

The fair-haired man smiled when he saw that Frederik had noticed the machine gun. Then he jerked his head back in the direction of the house and Frederik saw that there was another machine gun sticking out of the window of the rumpus room that was shut up during the winter. In that way they had most of the horizon covered, and the two men could also cover each other.

"What would you call people like us?" asked the Dane, as they went on over toward the barn. "Terrorists?"

Frederik nodded cautiously. He wasn't quite certain whether he understood what the man meant and, anyhow, he was trying to remember what it was he had forgotten.

"That's what they call us on television." said the man. "Elsewhere in the world they call us partisans. If not patriots. Do you know what that means?"

Frederik nodded.

"When Denmark was occupied and everyone could see who was going to win the war, then they called people like us freedom fighters," said the man.

Frederik nodded. What on earth was it he'd thought of just before he had spotted the machine guns?

"But Denmark isn't occupied now," said Frederik.

"That depends on how you look at it," said the man. "But even if you don't think Denmark is occupied, there are many other places in the world that *are* occupied, anyhow."

The man signaled up to the dark man, whose face had appeared at the window alongside the barrel of the machine gun. Then he went with Frederik ahead of him into the barn. Frederik thought about their plan. There was one dark man at each machine gun. The man in the mask was presumably indoors with his parents. And now he was being taken into the garage. Why? Would the man remain friendly? Or was something going to happen to him in the garage, where the others couldn't hear? It didn't seem so. The fair-haired man said:

"You wanted to know what was in the truck, didn't you?"

"Yes," said Frederik.

"Then you can have a look now. You'll read all about it in the papers tomorrow anyhow—if all goes well. If anything goes wrong, then neither you nor I will ever read a paper again."

The man opened the rear door of the truck. There was a smell of paint; the whole vehicle must have been painted recently. When Frederik's eyes had got used to the dark, he saw that there was a jeep inside, nose outward, and when he looked farther, he saw there was another jeep behind the first one. On the farthest jeep there was something which looked like a large firearm of some kind, but Frederik couldn't see it properly.

The man had not opened the truck in Frederik's honor, but to look into something. He hauled two broad metal sheets out, clearly for the jeeps to run down on. The man made sure they slid quickly and sat firmly. Then he called out something in English, the loft window above them opened, and the man behind the machine gun stuck his head out.

The two men chatted and laughed. Frederik thought that their laughter was a trifle nervous, but he himself was still wondering what it was that he couldn't remember.

He looked out over the yard. The snow looked lovely. For the first time this winter.

Day off for skiing, he thought.

Arim, Dan and he had agreed . . .

"Come on," said the man. "We must go now."

They went out into the yard. The fair man took off his spectacles because they had misted over. Frederik looked ahead; and then just as if you could make something happen just by thinking about it, he saw two dots on the road on their way out of the forest heading toward the house. He recognized them from a long way off, them and their bikes. It was Arim and Dan.

What would happen now?

The man went on endlessly polishing his glasses. From up

above came a small whistling signal and the man shoved his glasses back on with an incredibly quick movement. The next thing to happen was that Frederik was grabbed by the arm and hauled back into the barn with such force that he fell over. He looked up and saw the man swiftly but soundlessly closing the barn door.

Frederik had hit his head as he fell, and even before that it had felt heavy and fuzzy. It must be eleven o'clock and he had had no breakfast yet. He lay still, because the man had signaled him to, and because he now realized that Dan and Arim were also in great danger.

Frederik guessed that the two machine guns had been drawn slightly back, but that they were both now pointing at the front door. Any moment now, Arim and Dan would be ringing the bell, and his mother would be opening the door.

Because of the snow and the distance, they only just heard the sound of the bell ringing, and by straining, Frederik could just hear that someone was talking, but not what they were saying. The fair-haired man had placed himself so that he could see through a crack in the barn door, now and again glancing warningly at Frederik. He had his revolver out.

Much later, Frederik heard two bicycle bells ringing together. The fair-haired man hesitated for a few more minutes before cautiously opening the barn door slightly.

"All clear," he said. "It looks as if your mother found something sensible to say."

Frederik was ordered to go ahead, the man keeping a lookout all the time in case Dan and Arim should return. Suddenly he grasped Frederik's arm and said: "Had you thought about that? Had you thought about your school being given a day off for skiing?"

Frederik shook his head. It was too complicated to explain that he had not thought about it until it was too late. They went into the hall, where his mother was sitting looking very upset. The man in the mask had allowed Frederik's father to come out from the living room to comfort her.

"I'm afraid I made a mess of it," she said. "I said I hadn't sent for the doctor. They can check that."

"You mean the two kids might go off and get a doctor sent out here, Frederik?" said the man.

"Yes," said Frederik.

"Do *you* think your friends would use their day off to check whether a doctor was coming out here or not?"

"No," said Frederik.

"Neither do I," said the fair-haired man, smiling. "I don't think a doctor will come out here."

19

At last Frederik was given some breakfast, and his mother for once made coffee for him, so that he would wake up properly. His father sat meanwhile talking to the fair-haired man on the sofa, the two speaking politely to each other, almost like host and invited guest. But Frederik could hear that both of them were quite nervous.

"There's something I don't understand," said Frederik's father. "Why did you come as early as yesterday evening? Why not this evening?"

"We've made good use of the time," said the man. "First and foremost, with your assistance we've got the forest to ourselves. No forestry workers around. Last night we fixed the escape route. This afternoon we shall polish it a bit and also use the daylight for a few other small projects."

As if feeling very much at home, the fair-haired man said to Mrs. Poulsen:

"Could I possibly ask for a cup of coffee, now you've got the pot out? And I'm sure your husband would like one.

"Now we've got over the helicopter we had reckoned on," he went on. "When it gets a bit darker, we're going out to have a look at . . . at the shooting terrain. We're simply using today as a kind of dress rehearsal. It is *certainly* not a waste of time."

"No," said Frederik's father. "But you're running a risk."

"Oh, well," said the fair man. "Hitherto things have gone very well."

Frederik's mother poured the coffee.

"What's inside that moving van?" she asked.

The man shook his head with a smile. Frederik thought that now he knew more than his parents.

"Are you going to shoot Kreiser, like they shot Kennedy?" his mother said.

"Yes, we'll shoot him, but not like Kennedy. We haven't such good sharpshooters. So we're using a much bigger weapon."

"So you're going to kill several people?" she said, putting the coffeepot down because her hand was shaking so much.

"Yes," said the fair-haired man, looking down so they couldn't see the expression on his face.

Frederik was sent up to the bathroom to wash, and while he was there he heard a car drive into the yard. He looked out and saw it was Dr. Wechselmann, Dan's father. He heard some quiet orders from the stairs, and his father came into the bathroom.

"Frederik," he said. "I'm going to ask quite a lot of you. Go quickly into your room and put your pajamas on. Dr. Wechselmann has come. If he comes in to see you, the situation is as follows—your sister is ill, and we don't really know what's wrong with her. We have kept you home from school in case it's infectious. There's nothing wrong with you, so you don't have to act. And we're alone in the house, of course. Frederik, I hope you can manage all that.''

His father vanished again and Frederik sat down on the edge of his bed. His heart was thumping and he wasn't sure whether he could keep down the coffee he had just drunk. In front of him lay a horror comic. He wondered whether he would ever be able to read one again.

He heard Dan's father go into Margrethe's room with his parents. He knew that Margrethe was asleep, but that she probably didn't have a temperature. How would they manage that? The door of Margrethe's room opened and he heard his mother going into the bathroom. Frederik reckoned she was fetching a thermometer.

Was Margrethe sleeping so heavily that they couldn't even wake her?

And what would she say if they did wake her?

His mother came out of the bathroom and closed the door of Margrethe's room behind her.

Where were the four strangers *now*? And weren't they perhaps scared of what his mother and father might tell Dr. Wechselmann?

The door opened again and Frederik heard Margrethe whimpering a little as if she were so sleepy, she couldn't say anything that made sense. Frederik heard Dr. Wechselmann's voice.

''I can't make it out,'' he said. ''I'd have been much happier if she'd got a temperature. But I'll just have a look at Frederik.''

There was a knock on the door. Just as Dr. Wechselmann came in, Frederik realized that he couldn't keep the coffee down any longer. He managed to snatch up a bowl and then he was sick.

''Let's see now,'' said Dr. Wechselmann, taking his pulse and getting out the thermometer.

"Same thing again," said Dr. Wechselmann, "apart from the fact that Frederik has a very high pulse rate. But no temperature. This is nothing like either measles or German measles. In fact it's nothing like anything I've seen before."

"Gastroenteritis?" said Frederik's mother.

Dr. Wechselmann shook his head slowly.

"A virus of some kind?" said Frederik's father.

"Yes, perhaps," said Dr. Wechselmann. "Frederik's pulse might be high because he has just been sick. But what I don't understand at all is that it looks as if the children have two quite different illnesses. I mean, Frederik is wide awake . . ."

Now's the time to help a bit, thought Frederik, pretending to be hiding a yawn. Dr. Wechselmann stood looking at him.

"Well," he said. "I don't know. I can't make it out. But . . ."

"A virus?" repeated Frederik's father.

"Listen," said Dr. Wechselmann. "Let's leave it a while. I must be off to the hospital now. But I'd like to hear from you later today. Shall we say you ring the hospital if anything happens? And I'll keep Dan and Arim indoors until I've heard how things develop. It's a pity, just when it has at last snowed, but . . . well, we'll have a chat later on in the day."

Dr. Wechselmann took Frederik's pulse again before he left.

"Steady one hundred twenty," he said, shaking his head in a puzzled way. "Well, you're all right, Frederik, and I'll give your regards to Dan, shall I?"

"Yes, please," said Frederik, quite proud of himself over how he got his voice to sound as if he were slightly ill, but not bad enough to have to go to the hospital.

Over Dr. Wechselmann's shoulder he saw his father nodding in approval.

His parents went out behind Dr. Wechselmann and a little later Frederik heard the doctor's car start up and drive away.

There was a knock on the door and the fair-haired man came in.

"You managed that very well," he said. "That was a good idea being sick like that. Can you do that kind of thing to order?"

"No," said Frederik, bending over the bowl again, because there was more to come.

20

The telephone rang and Arim answered it.

It was Dan's father ringing from the Poulsens' house to say that Frederik and Margrethe appeared to have some virus or other.

"I know you'll be fed up about it, but I'd like you to stay indoors and not go around infecting a whole lot of others. Can I speak to Dan?"

He repeated the message to Dan and said he'd perhaps phone later.

"In return I promise I'll get you a day off school another time. And I think Arim's parents will agree to do the same."

Arim and Dan just sat there grumpily for a while. Then Dan suggested they should go out skiing all the same, but Arim wouldn't. He said he wanted to go down to the apartment and get some refreshments. After he had gone, Dan first looked at the photographs on the wall again. Then he went over to the big studio window and picked up the camera with the telescopic lens.

He got the Poulsen's house into the sights and just caught a glimpse of his father's car as it drove into the woods. It was fun with a telescopic lens on a camera like this. Just as the car came into view in the sight, he heard a click. He had pressed the shutter. He took the camera away from his eye to see if it had a film in it. It had.

Arim came back with his refreshments on a tray. Two bottles of beer, a packet of cigarettes, and some honey cakes.

"It's thawing," he said. "The others won't get much skiing."

Dan looked at the beers thoughtfully. He quite liked a little red wine, but he wasn't all that keen on beer. Oh, well, he would have to drink it, of course.

"I've just seen my father's car," he said.

He handed the camera to Arim, and after having kept on about they just mustn't touch that camera, Arim himself started looking through it.

"It's fun," he said. "You can almost see into the windows over there."

He opened the beers and they both lighted a cigarette, leaving the honey cakes for the time being. Arim put some wood on the fire in the tiled stove.

"All we need now is some music," he said.

He ran downstairs and brought up a transistor radio and they sat listening to some feeble afternoon concert as they smoked and drank. Dan decided he might be able to stand beer in the end. Finally he picked up the camera again.

"How does it actually work?" he asked.

They found out how you set the light meter in the sight. Dan went over to the window and again pointed the camera in the direction of the Poulsens' house. He adjusted it until the house stood out sharply in the little circle in the middle of the sight, which Arim said was the distance meter. Then he went and sat down by Arim to finish his beer.

"My father sounded peculiar," he said. "He usually knows what's wrong with people."

"Mrs. Poulsen was peculiar too."

"Do you think it's something dangerous? An epidemic or something?"

"Our lives are in danger," said Arim, laughing.

"There was something else I thought about," said Dan. "Ringo. He usually always comes belting out."

"He was down in the basement," said Arim. "I heard him whining."

"Ringo in the basement! D'you think they're scared they've got rabies?"

Arim laughed, but then started coughing because he was trying to inhale at the same time.

"Or cat flu," said Dan. "Anisette wasn't there either."

"Very peculiar," said Arim, swilling down the last of his beer. "I'll tell you something else peculiar that happened to me yesterday."

Arim told him about the two Englishmen he had first seen in the toy store, where they'd bought a doll and then tried on masks. Then he went on to say how he'd seen them again the next day, standing kicking the tire of a moving van. And how a taxi had finally driven up, with two men in it.

Dan, who had been thinking that he also had something peculiar to tell Arim, interrupted him.

"Was it a Mercedes?" he asked.

"Yes, but that wasn't peculiar."

"White?"

"Yes."

"Did it have two exhaust pipes?"

"I didn't notice that. It was an ordinary taxi."

"With a diesel engine?"

"I've no idea."

"Well," said Dan. "I saw a taxi on Monday, you see, which really was peculiar."

Dan told Arim about the taxi with the diesel plate and a

gasoline engine. It didn't seem to interest Arim, who asked whether he should go down and get two more beers.

Dan shook his head.

"The man driving the taxi—he didn't by any chance have a huge great wristwatch with lots of things on it, did he?"

"Yes," said Arim, who had suddenly remembered that indeed he had had just that, although he wasn't absolutely certain.

"Oh, well," said Dan. "Lots of people have got that kind of watch."

Neither of them could think of anything else peculiar and so finally once more, Dan picked up the camera and went over to the window. It was two o'clock and now you could almost see from the snow that the surface was poor.

Nothing was happening in the Poulsens' windows as far as Dan could see, so he moved the camera so that it was directed at the little clearing just behind the house. He knew Frederik's cave was just in front of it, but he couldn't see it. But he did see something else.

"There's Poulsen in his jeep," he said. "No," he went on. "That's not Poulsen's jeep."

"What is it then?" said Arim, yawning.

"It's an Italian jeep. It's stopped now."

There was a small click and Arim jumped up.

"You idiot, you; you pressed the shutter," he cried.

But Dan was just standing staring through the camera.

"It's not Poulsen's," he said. "It's an Italian jeep. It's one of those that Fiat make. And it's got no number plates on. And . . ."

"Yes," said Arim.

At that moment, the studio door jerked open and Hanna, Arim's sister, came rushing in.

"What on earth are you two doing in here?" she said.

21

"Because you were so clever at acting sick, you're going to be given a little ride."

Frederik knew perfectly well he was to be hostage again.

"Your son's in the best of hands, as long as nothing unexpected happens," the fair-haired man said to Frederik's parents.

Then he pushed Frederik ahead of him and they went out to the barn, where the man stood listening for a moment before opening the door. Inside the barn, he let down the back flap of the truck and pulled out the two steel sheets like a ramp. Then he drove the first jeep out into the yard, then the second one.

The first jeep was an ordinary jeep with number plates. The second had no number plates and was green rather than brown. Frederik noticed that it had no jeep label on it, but "Fiat." He also saw that six rocket missiles were mounted on the back of it. The back had been turned into a kind of launching pad. The six missiles lay side by side, each in its little holder, like a section of a pipe. Each was about half a meter long and had fins. There was a seat on the back of the jeep, too, and in front of it a kind of instrument panel with buttons and indicators.

The fair-haired man drove the ordinary jeep back into the barn and then stood looking up at the sky.

"Do you think any more helicopters will come over today?" he asked.

Frederik didn't know what to say. He was hungry again because of bringing up all his breakfast, but at the same time he was feeling slightly sick.

"Well," said the man. "We'll keep in under the trees. Jump in."

Frederik got in beside the man and they drove behind the barn and in among the trees. A little later they stopped, only the nose of the jeep showing. They could see down to where Frederik's cave lay below a couple of pine trees, and the man smiled, pointing ahead.

"There's a cave down there which I suppose you made," he said. "We saw it one day when we were taking photographs out here."

Frederik nodded.

"Who knows—perhaps we'll find a use for it," said the man.

He looked at his watch.

"It's a little lighter than I reckoned with," he said.

Frederik followed the direction of his look. Where they were, they couldn't see the motorway, only hear it. But if they drove down to the little hillock just behind his cave, he knew they would be able to see the motorway just where it crossed the river at Lundtofte. They could aim at the cars as they approached.

Just in front of the hillock there was a group of trees. If they could get from the clearing over to them, they would again be out of sight of any helicopter.

"Are those rockets on the back?" asked Frederik.

The man thought for a moment before replying.

"Why shouldn't I tell you?" he said. "We're leaving this jeep behind anyhow. So there's no point in it remaining a mystery."

He lighted a cigarette and suddenly held the packet out to Frederik.

"Do you smoke?" he said, without a trace of a smile.

Frederik shook his head, feeling sick.

"Yes," said the man. "They're rockets. I presume you also want to know what they're called. They're called Cobras."

The man inhaled and blew a smoke ring.

"A Cobra for Kreiser," he said.

"How do you shoot things like that?" Frederik asked.

"You take aim and simply send off the rockets, and then an expert directs them from here. And do you know how he does that?"

Frederik shook his head.

"There's a kind of thread or wire in them. The steering is electronic. So there's always a link with them from here, until you're certain they're going to hit. Then they bore their way through armored plate up to thirty millimeters thick and explode."

"Why have you got six?" asked Frederik.

"Because we hope to hit six cars. We can't be certain which one of them Kreiser will be in, can we?"

"What happens in the six cars?" asked Frederik, feeling sick again.

"Nothing very nice," said the man. "We'll try and hit the first car first and then the whole motorcade will stop. Then it's just a question of hitting the rest afterward."

"Will they all die?" asked Frederik.

"As many as necessary," replied the man.

He looks so tired, Frederik thought. And his hands were shaking so much that he kept dropping ash onto his knees when he took the cigarette out of his mouth.

Frederik looked ahead and saw the top stories of apartment houses on the other side of the motorway. As far as he could see there was no light on at Arim's. They were probably all out skiing.

"It's dark enough now, I should think," he said.

It was half past three and it didn't seem all that dark to Frederik. But of course, it wasn't all that far from the clearing to the trees where they were to stop. And there was no sound of a helicopter.

"Who would be able to see us?" said the fair-haired man, flicking away his cigarette end.

He noticed that Frederik was looking over toward the buildings on the other side of the motorway.

"Yes," he said. "If someone over there had a very good pair of binoculars. At this very moment. But that's not likely, is it? And what would he see? A jeep "

"With rockets on the back," said Frederik.

"Yes," said the man. "If he had very good binoculars. That's the smallest chance I've ever taken in my life."

He started the jeep and drove over to the trees, where they were once again sheltered.

"What do you think of the view?" he said to Frederik.

They looked down toward the motorway, along which Henry Kreiser would be driving at eleven o'clock the next morning.

22

"Yes," said Hanna. "That's a jeep. And so what?"

She had spent ages ranting at Arim and Dan for smoking, and for drinking beer, and for messing around in the studio, where they were not allowed, and for messing up the tiled stove and for playing with that hideously expensive camera.

"It's not a jeep," said Dan. "It's a Fiat."

Hanna had taken about ten minutes to cool down. Not until then had they managed to get her to pick up the camera and look over toward the Poulsens'.

"All right," said Hanna. "Then it's a Fiat? So . . ."

She stopped.

"It's coming out," she said. "There are two people in it."

"Press the shutter," cried Arim.

"Why not? You've already wrecked the film."

There was a click. Arim and Dan pressed their noses against the windowpane on each side of Hanna.

"There's something on the back," cried Dan.

"Yes," said Hanna. "It did look peculiar. There, now, it's gone behind those trees."

All three of them looked. The light had begun to fade.

"What the hell was that on the back?" said Dan.

"And why are they stopping in there under the trees?" said Arim.

"Who was in it?" asked Dan.

"It looked like a man and a boy," said Hanna. "Mr. Poulsen and Frederik, I suppose."

"Frederik's ill and has to stay indoors," said Arim.

"You two are always making mysteries out of things," said Hanna, putting down the camera. But then she picked it up again.

"Is it coming out again?" asked Dan.

"No. But it'll soon be too dark to see anything."

"What the hell was that on the back?" Dan said again.

"I don't know," said Hanna. She paused. "You know— Frederik's father—Mr. Poulsen—"

"Yes."

"I've never seen him. Is he fair-haired?"

"No, he certainly isn't," said Arim.

"Does he wear glasses?"

"No."

"Well," said Hanna. "I might have got it wrong, of course."

Arim knew his sister. You had to contradict her now.

"Yes, you got it wrong," he said. "The man wasn't fair and he didn't have glasses on. And there was nothing peculiar at all about what was on the back of the jeep."

Hanna began to wind the film. Her mother wouldn't be back for another hour, and it would be even longer before her father came.

"You two'll have to pay for a new film," she said, as she took the film out of the camera and went into the darkroom with it. "*No* more beer, and *no* more cigarettes, and clear up in here, and keep away from the darkroom while I develop this."

While Arim and Dan were clearing up, they heard the sound of a helicopter and they rushed over to the window. It was flying low along the motorway, over on the other side.

"The cops again," said Dan.

Over on the other side of the motorway, the fair-haired man grasped Frederik by the back of the neck and forced him down into the jeep, at the same time crouching down himself.

"Just as well we got in under the trees," the man said, when the helicopter had passed. "And just as well it didn't come a quarter of an hour ago. Well, there are limits to what they can see. But they'll come back, and we'll be the ones who've vanished in the meantime."

He turned the jeep around and drove without lights up to the edge of the wood again. One of the dark-haired men was waiting for them. He had opened the door of the barn, and he brushed his hand across his forehead to show how nervous he'd been. Just as the fair man switched off the engine, they heard the helicopter approaching again.

"You'd think the Danish police were expecting something to happen tomorrow," the man said.

With Frederik in front of him, he went into the house. Frederik's mother was making tea, and in some ways everything seemed quite normal. His father was sitting in the living room with a book and Margrethe had awakened and was sitting sleepily playing with the big doll that said ma-ma when you put it down.

Frederik's mother came in with the tray and while Frederik handed around the cups, she lighted the fire.

"There's nothing against us having a cozy time," she said,

trying to smile at Frederik and Margrethe. The door behind her was ajar and Frederik knew that the man in the mask was out there.

"No," said his father, putting down his book. "Nothing except the thought that a lot of people are going to die tomorrow."

When they'd finished tea, it was quite dark outside, and the man in the mask sent Frederik upstairs to his room to rest, locking the door behind him. He sat on the edge of his bed looking at the things the man had searched through and left lying on the floor.

Among them, he saw his flashlight. Absentmindedly, he picked it up and went over to the window. He stood there for a long time, looking out into the dark.

Over in Arim's father's studio, Dan and Arim were waiting for Hanna to reappear from the darkroom. She came at last with a negative in her hand. She turned on the projector, which threw its light onto the wall, and switched off the studio light. Then she swiftly put the negative into a frame and slipped it into the projector.

The picture had been successful and was sharp and clear. It showed a strange-looking jeep with a battery of rockets on the back. The rockets weren't very big, but there were six of them. At the wheel was a stranger, his hair short and fair, and he was wearing steel-rimmed glasses. Beside him sat Frederik, Dan and Arim's best friend.

23

Twenty minutes later, Hanna, Arim, and Dan were almost quarreling.

"You've been looking at too much television," said Hanna. "Terrorists in Narum. All right, they *look* like rockets, but...."

"They *are* rockets," said Dan.

"All right, let's say they are, but then it's probably a Danish policeman in plain clothes or something like that."

"They *are* rockets. And it's not a proper jeep. And don't forget we were told that Frederik had to stay indoors. And how could one ever protect Henry Kreiser with rockets?"

"Well," said Hanna. "If...."

She stopped.

"And they waited until they thought there were no more helicopters," said Arim.

"*They?*" said Hanna. "I saw only one man."

"I bet you anything there are more in the house," said Arim. "And I think those two Englishmen I saw in the toy store and then by that moving van—I think they...."

"Thanks," said Hanna. "No more cops-and-robbers stories, please. Tell me, just how many beers did you two drink this afternoon?"

"One each," said Arim. "And you've got to take this seriously."

Both Dan and Arim were a bit fed up that Hanna was involved in the whole thing, but they were pleased too, because who else would have developed the film? It was just that they both thought that boys ought to be better than girls at such things.

"All right, then," said Hanna. "The Poulsens' house is

seething with terrorists who want to murder Henry Kreiser. What do we do in such a situation? We show the picture to Dad and Mum. And what would they do? They'd go to the police. Then the police could soon find out if that jeep is anything that they have to do something about or not.''

Dan and Arim looked at each other. Dan was the first to object.

''And what would the police do? Rush over there with motorbikes and helicopters and tear gas and machine guns.''

Arim went on:

''The police would save Kreiser and all those other high-ups in the cars at all costs. At the cost of Frederik's and Margrethe's and their parents' lives, too.''

''If all your fancy theories are correct,'' said Hanna. ''Anyhow, the police would make sure . . .''

She was interrupted by Arim, who was looking out of the studio window over toward the Poulsens' house.

''Hand me the camera,'' he said. ''I want to use it as binoculars.''

''What's happening?''

''It looks as if Frederik is signaling to us with his flashlight.''

Hanna reluctantly handed Arim the camera.

''Yes. Gosh, it's Frederik, and he is flashing!'' said Arim. ''Three green. Come on, we must go down.''

''Flashing?'' said Hanna. ''What on earth are you blathering about?''

Arim rushed down the stairs, with Dan behind him, and as Hanna came after them, Dan explained to her what he knew about Arim and Frederik's Morse code system.

The door to the apartment wasn't locked, and Arim rushed straight in. In the hall stood his mother.

''Where on earth have you been?'' she said. ''And what about wiping your feet before . . .''

She caught sight of Dan and Hanna, hard on Arim's heels.

Arim left it to them to keep her there while he ran into his room, snatched up his flashlight and the Morse code and climbed out through the window onto the balcony. Behind him, he heard his mother asking Dan and Hanna if they happened to know what had happened to two beers, a packet of cigarettes, and a transistor radio.

Frederik wasn't flashing any longer. Arim sent out his starting signal, three green flashes. Perhaps Frederik was still there looking out, even if he had stopped flashing. Arim signaled three greens again. He heard Dan coming into his room, while out in the hall Hanna was still trying to answer her mother's questions and keep her there.

"Give me pen and paper," he said to Dan.

Frederik was replying. Three green flashes. Then the signal that meant: *I'm going over to Morse.*

There was nothing for it but to write the signals down. Arim was much too bad at Morse to try anything else. He could neither "read" the signals just like that, nor reply to them. If Frederik had something important to say, Arim hoped that he was going to start at once, before his mother put her oar in, and that wouldn't be long, it seemed, as Hanna couldn't hold her back much longer.

Frederik seemed to be flashing only three words. They weren't wholly according to the Morse code, but they had agreed that they could flash red and green once between each word to separate them more definitely. Although Arim had no idea what the words he received were, he signaled their homemade *received and understood* signal back, hoping it wasn't a lie.

Arim could hear his mother on her way into the room behind him, and he flashed red-red-white-green-red, which as far as he could remember in the confusion meant *interference from parents*. Then he hurriedly sent a signal white-white-green-white, which, as far as he remembered, meant *stay there and wait*. Then he climbed back through the window into his room again, while pushing the piece of paper into his pants pocket. "What's going on here?'' said his mother.

It took ten minutes and multitudes of promises to replace the cigarettes, the beers, clear up the studio, and lay the table to get her out of the room. She didn't look angry; on the contrary, it ended with her laughing and saying that Arim and Dan should be allowed to be a bit "mysterious,'' as they'd been cheated of their skiing.

Dan ran up to the attic and tidied up a bit, while Hanna ran down to the shop and bought two beers and a packet of cigarettes. Arim stood over by the window, opened it and signaled again to Frederik, but there were no more signals in reply.

Arim sat down at the table and started writing out the three words with the help of the Morse alphabet. The first word came to: *Hastoge.*

The next word was: *Kreyser.*

But the third was the strangest: *Cobra.*

Dan came in, and then Hanna a moment later. They leaned over his shoulder and read the three words Arim had written down.

"*Hastoge,*'' said Dan. "What on earth's that? It must be *hostage.*''

"And the next must be *Kreiser,*'' said Hanna.

The third word they couldn't make out at all.

"Cobra,'' said Dan. "That's a snake.''

"Frederik and the others have been taken hostage,'' said Arim. "The whole thing is about Kreiser. And he's to be killed by a cobra!''

"By Agent Double-oh-seven,'' said Hanna, but no one laughed.

There was a knock on the door.

"Come and lay the table,'' said Arim's mother. "Dan's father has come to fetch Dan.''

24

The key turned in the door behind Frederik. He had to get the flashlight out of the way and he could find only one hiding place—down behind the radiator. He had to push to get the fat flashlight right down. The switch rubbed against the wall and the light went on. The door behind him opened.

It was the man in the mask.

So long as the light was on in the room, perhaps the man wouldn't notice the light shining behind the radiator. But the man was standing with his hand on the switch.

"You are wanted downstairs," he said.

As always, Frederik had to go first. The man in the mask stood in the doorway, looking around Frederik's room. He hadn't turned the light out yet. Finally he turned around and switched it off. He had his back to the room as he switched it off, and didn't see the flashlight stuck behind the radiator, its light shining on the wall.

But it was still shining. And when Frederik went back to his room, he would be escorted by someone. It would be dark in the room—apart from the flashlight.

Frederik thought about how strange it was that his random signals had been seen over at Arim's. Arim could have had no idea that he had been standing there. They hadn't agreed on a time. But Arim had perhaps thought that Frederik was bored because he "was ill."

Frederik was sorry he had tried to signal a message in Morse about Kreiser and all that. Arim was bad at reading Morse and hadn't an earthly chance of understanding the message Frederik had tried to send. Frederik had risked his own and his family's life with that wretched message, which Arim wouldn't have the least chance of understanding. And now the flashlight was lying there shining behind the radiator in the dark room. Just how stupid can you get?

Down in the living room, Frederik's mother and father were sitting down and the fair-haired Dane was standing by the fire.

Cobra, thought Frederik. How could just that one word say anything to Arim?

"Sit down," said the Dane. "There are one or two things we must talk about before we turn in."

Turn in, thought Frederik. It's not even six o'clock. At that moment, the telephone rang.

The fair-haired man nodded at Frederik's mother, who got up and picked up the receiver. They could hear quite clearly that it was Otto—Frederik's father's shooting companion, who, Frederik's mother said, was responsible for at least half their telephone bill.

"I'm alone," she said very quickly, "and I'm just cooking our meal."

That didn't stop Otto for one minute.

"Listen, Otto," said Frederik's mother. "I've got something in the oven, which I must take out . . ."

"I can smell something burning," said Frederik's father, half-aloud. "I wonder if something *is* burning in the kitchen."

"Otto," said Frederik's mother. "I must run. Call back? No, preferably tomorrow morning. No, no, later on in the day. It'd be better if . . ."

Otto had more to say.

"No," said Frederik's mother. "It's no use just turning down the oven. Otto, you must phone another time. Good-bye, now."

"He was offended," said Frederik's mother. "He slammed the receiver down without saying good-bye."

"You needn't have made it so brief for my sake," said the Dane. "I suppose *he* won't think of looking in now?"

96

"It didn't sound like it," said Frederik's mother.

"If so, then we'll wake you up and it'll be tough," said the fair-haired man. "Or we'll pretend that there is no one at home."

"Wake us?" said Frederik's father. "We aren't going to bed yet, are we?"

"Yes," said the man, moving away from the fire. "I thought all four of you ought to have a long, calm night, so that you're quite rested tomorrow."

At a signal, one of the dark-haired men came in. He was carrying a tray with four glasses of juice on it and a glass of tablets.

"What would happen if we refused to play with you any more?" said Frederik's father.

"You will 'play with' us all the same. If any one of you does anything thoughtless, then we'll be forced to put the silencer on a revolver now, Mr. Poulsen. But what*ever* you do, you won't be able to save Henry Kreiser's life with your own. Heroics are wasted now."

"And what if I tell you now," said Frederik's father, "that we're expecting guests this evening?"

"Then I wouldn't believe you, Mr. Poulsen. But if the worst comes to the worst, we could also take your guests as hostages. You must try to reconcile yourself to the fact that there is nothing whatsoever you can do."

"It's not Kreiser so much," said Frederik's father. "He has always known that he is running a risk. It's all the others, all those innocent people. This could affect ordinary people who just happen to be on the motorway tomorrow morning."

"It could, yes," said the Dane. "There's nothing we can do about that. But in the long run, we reckon that our action will *save* thousands of lives. Ordinary people's too."

"The long run," said Frederik's father. "How? Isn't Kreiser a mediator for peace?"

"We don't believe that any longer. And we prefer a swift settlement to an endless, bloody, so-called cease-fire. It is precisely *we* who are getting tired of the long run, Mr. Poulsen. Take these tablets now, so at least the time can be short for *you.*"

Frederik couldn't really understand what the two men were talking about, and he was thinking all the time about his flashlight stuck behind the radiator.

"You others, too," said the fair-haired man, pulling out his revolver to show that they should get a move on. They swallowed their sleeping tablets, two for Frederik and Margrethe, four for their mother and father.

"And up to bed," said the man. "Tonight the family will sleep together for the sake of order. In your bedroom," he added, turning to the parents. "We'll move the children in."

Frederik noticed his heart thumping slightly less violently. No one would go to his room now.

All four of them went upstairs. Margrethe looked as if she had completely ceased to understand what was happening, and as if she were too tired to cry, but halfway up the stairs, she took Frederik's hand and he, too, was pleased to have someone's hand to hold.

The door to Frederik's room was not opened. His last thought before he fell asleep with his father and mother and sister was that the flashlight battery would probably run out during the night.

25

Arim sneezed.

"There you are," said his mother out in the hall. "Now you've gone and caught a cold."

Arim had looked up "cobra" in the encyclopedia. It couldn't be anything else but a snake.

"What shall we do now?" he said to Hanna.

"There's only one thing to do," she said. "We tell Mother and Dad everything we know. Let's go up and get the photograph."

The two of them hadn't had a chance to talk to each other during dinner. Arim had looked at his watch a hundred times.

"We're going up to the studio," said Hanna, when her mother said that they were not to go out that evening.

Their father was up in the studio, squatting down trying to light the fire in the stove.

"What a mess you made here this afternoon," he said. "I should really be cross with you. You've exposed a whole film with nothing on it. What've you been up to, Hanna?"

"There were a couple of pictures on it," said Hanna.

"Were there?" said her father. "I didn't see them. There was so much rubbish lying about here, I used it all to light the fire. Sorry if I happened to destroy any photographic masterpieces."

Hanna and Arim hunted for the negative they had had in the projector that afternoon. It was gone.

"You might as well stop looking," said their father. "I've thrown all of your junk out. And we must have some other arrangement in future, Hanna. The stove's in a dreadful mess, and that's dangerous, too."

A little later, Arim and Hanna were down in Arim's room again.

"Without the photograph, they'd never believe that cops-and-robbers stuff," said Hanna.

"And if they had the photograph, they'd ring the police, and would the police be able to decide whether Frederik and his family should survive, or Henry Kreiser?" said Arim, thinking about the two policemen he had seen up on the motorway the day before. He could hardly think of anyone he would be more reluctant to leave that decision to.

"Not just Kreiser," said Hanna. "If there really *were* six rockets on that jeep . . ."

"But we saw them."

"If only we had that photograph still."

Arim tried to signal over to Frederik, but there was no one signaling back. Hostages, Kreiser, Cobra, he thought.

"We could bike over there and . . ."

"And what? Can one person on a bike release four hostages?"

"You could come, too."

"Thanks a million."

"We could telephone," said Arim. "If only Dan was here, at least."

"You mean it's better for two people to phone, than one?" said Hanna. "If all this isn't something we're imagining—then who'll answer the phone over there?"

"Well, let's tell Mother and Dad."

"They'd either laugh their heads off or call the police."

"We could phone Dan."

"Yes," said Hanna. "I think we should do that. But listen—let's leave it, now. Kreiser is not coming until eleven o'clock tomorrow. Perhaps the visit'll be canceled. Perhaps they'll take another route."

"Do you think we ought to leave it?" said Arim uncertainly.

"Yes," said Hanna, but she didn't look as if she had had the most brilliant idea in the whole world.

On Hegn Road, Dan was standing in his father's study with the telephone receiver in his hand. He could hear that his parents were watching television in the living room. He was trying to phone Arim, but the number was busy. Then he dialed Narum police station, trying to make his voice as deep as possible.

"This is an anonymous warning," he said. "Someone will murder Henry Kreiser tomorrow with some rockets."

"May we have your name, young man?" said the policeman at the other end.

Dan put the receiver down slowly. That had been an exceptionally hopeless idea.

A moment later Arim phoned and told Dan what he and Hanna had agreed on.

"You know," said Hanna, after Arim had spoken to Dan. "I think I've got a plan . . ."

Cobra, thought Dan. What the hell does Cobra mean?

THURSDAY

26

Frederik was awakened by someone pulling and tugging at him. It was one of the dark-haired men. The other one was standing with Margrethe in his arms, trying to wake their parents up.

It was still dark as they were ordered below. Margrethe opened her eyes, but looked no more awake. Her mother examined her as she lay there in the dark man's arms.

"You'll kill her if you give her any more of those pills," she said to the fair-haired man, who had appeared in the doorway out to the yard.

"She won't die that way," he said. "And if all goes well, she won't die at all."

"*Well*," repeated Frederik's mother, beginning to cry.

"Yes," said the fair-haired man. "Well."

They all put on warm clothes in the living room. Then they had to walk ahead of the fair-haired man through the yard and down the slope toward the motorway. Frederik guessed that it was about seven o'clock. As he walked, he glanced at Margrethe, who was still lying there with her eyes open, but quite expressionless.

How would she think back on all this, if she ever got a chance to think about it all? And how would he himself think back on it? Frederik reckoned that his sister would remember almost nothing, as she had spent so much of the time asleep.

But he? If he survived? Arim would witness that he'd been bright enough to signal with his flashlight. Bright enough or crazy enough. Perhaps he shouldn't boast all that much about it.

They came to the little clump of trees that lay just behind Frederik's cave and the hummock in the field. The two jeeps were there, the one Frederik had ridden in—with the missiles on the back—and the other one. Both could well be used as escape vehicles, thought Frederik. But how far?

How far could you drive a jeep with a rocket launching pad on the back along roads seething with police?

Frederik's father had obviously been thinking the same thing, because he said to the fair-haired man:

"I presume you have a more ordinary vehicle somewhere?"

"You can rest assured on that point," the man replied, smiling. "We aren't amateurs."

It was cold and clear, several degrees below zero. The last stars faded away, and through the bare forest they could see the morning sky glowing red.

The fair-haired man lighted a cigarette.

"As you see, Mr. Poulsen, there's room for eight people in the escape vehicles."

"You promised us . . ." began Frederik's mother.

"That we wouldn't do anything unnecessary," said the fair-haired man. "We'll keep that promise."

Frederik looked at the six rockets. The jeep was already facing in the right direction. It just needed driving a little farther on, he knew, before it would have a clear view down onto the motorway, down to the bridge over the river.

"But . . ." began Frederik's mother.

The fair-haired man hushed her. A helicopter was approaching. It was flying quite high up and was struck by the first rays of the morning sun, flashing in the sunlight like a great red insect.

When Frederick looked at his mother again, he saw she had fallen to her knees, as if she were praying with her eyes closed. He had never seen her like that before.

On the other side of the motorway, Arim and Hanna also heard the helicopter. Neither of them had found it particularly difficult to persuade their parents that they were not feeling well enough to go to school. Their mother was teaching in the morning and had left at half past seven. Shortly afterward, their father had left too, as he was going to take photographs of the big event of the day.

When Arim heard his father's car start up and drive away, he thought that was the last chance of any sensible adult being mixed up in all this. He wasn't at all certain whether he was pleased or not.

"I don't think the plan's good enough," he said to Hanna.

"You thought so last night."

"Yes, but we're taking much too great a risk. And it's much too simple."

"Good plans are always simple," said Hanna, looking uncertain.

"A bike," said Arim. "Stopping Kreiser with a bike! What'll happen? They'll push us aside and go on. We'll just give that Kreiser two more minutes to live."

"No," said Hanna. "We'll stop the whole motorcade. Then those people over at the Poulsens' will see and abandon their plans."

"The more I think about it, the more feeble it sounds," said Arim. "And dangerous. What if one of the police loses his head and starts shooting at us? It's a rotten plan."

Hanna looked as if she agreed with him.

"Phone Dan," she said.

Arim phoned, but there was no reply. Arim began to feel really bad. First Mother had gone, then Dad, and now they couldn't get hold of Dan. And at the same time, neither Hanna nor he had any faith in the plan they had made the night before.

"Okay, make a better plan," said Hanna.

THURSDAY

It was nine o'clock and she listened to the news on the radio. Kreiser had arrived at Kastrup Airport, said the announcer, and would shortly be driving to Fredensborg Palace to have lunch with the Queen and Prince Henrik.

"I'll phone the police," said Arim. "I'd have done that last night if you hadn't had your brilliant plan."

Arim had already lifted the telephone receiver when the doorbell rang. It was Dan. His cheeks were red, and he was so out of breath that it was some time before he could say anything.

"Phew," he said finally. "It began well enough—skipping school. But then Mother suddenly decided that she wanted to stay at home and make camomile tea for me and all sorts of things. In the end, I had to creep out and pinch my clothes, and then get out through the window. If the telephone rings, then I'm not here. Now listen . . ."

Dan stopped and listened; a helicopter was again on its way over above them.

"Well, I biked out to Brede and Orholm and all over there. I thought that if they're using jeeps to get through the forest, then they must have an escape car parked somewhere. And do you know what?"

Arim and Hanna shook their heads

Dan drew it out deliberately, although they were in a hurry.

"A six-cylinder Mercedes which goes at two hundred kilometers an hour! But which is rigged up to look like a slow old diesel taxi! It was parked in Ravnholm by that closed factory, just where *I* would have put it. I went far enough into the forest to be able to see that they have arranged the escape route a bit. They've put some boards over a ditch."

"Did you puncture the tires?" asked Arim.

"Are you crazy? Puncture them. That's the most dangerous thing you can do. Then they'd begin to shoot. Then they'd get the jitters. Then they'd lose their heads and heaven knows what else.''

"How many people can they get into that car?'' asked Hanna.

"Five, at the most six. Certainly not eight.''

"So they're not taking the Poulsens with them as hostages,'' said Arim.

"They might have other vehicles. You *could* get eight people into the Mercedes, I suppose. It would be lunatic to try to stop them getting away. With or without the Poulsens.''

Hanna and Arim nodded. They told Dan about the plan which had seemed so good the night before. Dan didn't think it was all that good, either. But there was something else that was annoying him.

"Cobra,'' he said. "There was a car called the Cobra once, but it can't be that. In our encyclopedia it just says something about a snake.''

"In ours, too,'' said Arim.

"Can I look?''

Dan saw that it just mentioned cobra snakes. Then he asked for the index volume, which was the index for all the other volumes.

"Coblenz, Cobnut, Cobol, Cobra,'' he read out aloud. "Wait, look at this! Snake, it says. And then it says *missile*. Rocket, hell. Cobra rocket, see volume nineteen, page four hundred and eight.''

All three of them sat there reading the encyclopedia article. The Cobra rocket was, they read, a German antitank rocket with a range of one English mile, or sixteen hundred meters.

"Do you know what?'' said Dan. "I think that's what *I* would use, if I were them.''

"Yes,'' said Arim. "But how does that help us?''

Hanna raised both her arms to show she was thinking and was about to have another idea.

"Listen," she said. "Who are we *really* trying to contact now? The police? No. They'll just get—at best—Kreiser to safety, and that won't in the least help Frederik and the others. So..."

Hanna stood up and looked around the room, as if she were about to hit on something important.

"So it's those people over at the Poulsens' we must warn. We'll just telephone over there and say one word—Cobra. Then they'll know..."

"It'd be Frederik's mother or father who'd answer the phone," said Dan. "If they haven't already been sent out of the house and down to the jeep with the rockets."

"Just that one word," said Hanna. "Cobra. If we could in some way or other..."

Arim got up quickly, his cheeks as red as Dan's.

"Cobra," he said. "I'll fix that. You two had better go and try stopping Kreiser with a bike, but I'll personally see to it that Kreiser and the people over at the Poulsens' and the police and the whole of the rest of Narum will see the word 'Cobra.' As long as there's a bit of wind."

"Wind?" said Dan and Hanna together.

"Yes," said Arim. "Wind."

27

The sun rose above the edge of the forest, no longer large and red, but small and white. The high-tension wires which ran above the small group of trees crackled as they always did in frosty weather.

Frederik saw how his father kept looking to see what the time was and then remembering that he had not been allowed to take his watch with him. Frederik had often looked in the same way at a watch that wasn't there.

Three of the men were now standing together under the trees. The jeep with the rockets was standing farthest back for the time being, ready to be driven forward. One of the dark-haired men had tested both jeeps to see if they would start and was now sitting on the back of the jeep with the rockets, apparently giving the firing mechanism a final test. He had put aside two weapons, a revolver and a rifle.

The man in the mask was walking backward and forward between the jeeps. Once he had crept quite a distance forward with his binoculars and had returned smiling. Frederik thought only his mouth was smiling, as his eyes were of course invisible.

The fair-haired man was speaking English into a walkie-talkie. Frederik did not understand the orders, but presumed that the other dark-haired man was receiving them. Or had the four men communications with someone else in quite a different place?

The three men had changed out of their black track suits into green overalls, and they were wearing helmets. They had gas masks round their necks. On the back of the jeep with number plates lay a half-open sack of clothes. To his surprise, Frederik saw that on the top layer was a taxi driver's cap.

''If I were Kreiser . . .'' Frederik's father began. The fair man looked at him with interest.

''Then I wouldn't take the route that had been announced,'' Frederik's father went on.

''But then the helicopters and police directing things would be elsewhere, wouldn't they?'' said the Dane.

''Anyhow,'' said Frederik's father. ''I'd come at a different time than that announced.''

''That's just what Henry Kreiser's going to do, too,'' said the fair-haired man. "He's coming ten minutes early, if you want to know."

Frederik's father looked down at the ground, and for the first time Frederik realized that his father would probably think back on this time as a defeat or something like that, if he survived. But what kind of defeat? Frederik didn't think his father could have done anything else apart from what he had done—which was nothing.

The fair-haired man took a message over the walkie-talkie, just one single word, then signaled to the dark man and got into the jeep with the rockets. The dark man got in the seat on the back and adjusted what looked like a pair of binoculars.

The fair man started the engine. The man in the mask fetched some ropes from the other jeep and the next few minutes were taken up with tying up Frederik's, his father's, his mother's, and his sister's hands behind their backs.

Frederik wondered if they would be gagged, too, so that they couldn't shout, but that was clearly not to be so. Neither were they blindfolded. But they were ordered to shelter behind the jeep with the number plates. To avoid thinking about all sorts of things, Frederik thought about what he would say about all this should he be lucky enough to survive. He wished he had someone's hand to hold, but his hands were tied behind his back.

On the other side of the motorway, Arim waved one last time to Dan and Hanna before they moved out of sight. They had hurriedly cycled off toward Lundtofte, as Hanna had said that it just *might* be that the motorcade would come earlier than they had reckoned.

Arim hadn't so far to go as they had, only as far as the slope in front of the shopping center. He was cycling along with one hand on the handlebars, a kite under his free arm. It was the yellow cross-kite, and with a paintbrush from his mother's paintbox and some blue paint, he had inscribed one single word in as large letters as there was room for on the kite.

The word was "Cobra."

The fluttering pennants on the top of the shopping center told him that the direction of the wind was right and that there was a good breeze. He stopped at a place where he calculated he could get up most speed to get the kite going and get air beneath it. But he would have liked to have someone to help, as the kite was really far too big to be set up by one person.

Arim was no longer at all certain that his plan was a good one. They would see the kite if he got it up at all, and then what? They would read the word, but why would that stop them from firing off the rockets? Or stop them from using the Poulsen family as hostages and perhaps killing them one by one, to save themselves?

Wouldn't they just be confused? And do something confused—if they didn't laugh at the funny joke that the word "Cobra" happened to be on a kite some boy or other had sent up?

The police and the Home Guard would also see the kite. But of course they wouldn't understand the meaning of the word "Cobra."

And Dan and Hanna's plan—that was even worse. If they ever found the courage to carry it through.

Arim looked up toward the bridge. A helicopter came into sight behind it and started coming toward him. Well, for the time being they couldn't see that he was about to get a kite up, and they flew over him at quite a height. The kite line, which he had wound tightly onto a spindle, looked good and was not tangled.

From where he was standing he could see that the traffic was thinning out up on the bridge over the motorway. The access road from Narum looked as if it were blocked, either by the police or a traffic jam, but no cars were coming down it from the Copenhagen direction.

He could just see a group of people waving flags up on the bridge, probably his own class and his teacher. The next time he looked up there, it seemed as if the police had moved them away from the railing. Arim looked at his watch. Quarter to eleven. So it was time; the agreement was that the kite should go up in time for the terrorists to have a reasonable respite to reconsider the situation and perhaps abandon the Poulsens. Arim no longer believed in the idea for one moment, but he had to go through with what they had agreed to do.

He began running. It was difficult without someone else to hold the line while he ran. He stumbled and the kite fell down into the long grass, so that the line was covered with rime frost when he began the second attempt.

It worked. The kite rose and he had a good hold on the line. The wind direction was right higher up, too, and the kite sailed over toward the motorway, and toward the camping site on the other side of the Poulsens' house. Arim stood with the spindle in both hands and let the line unroll by itself. It was pulling well.

All in all, he had five hundred meters of line, and when that was all used up, he would simply let the kite go. Then he would bike after Dan and Hanna and see if there was anything he could help them with.

The kite was now a hundred meters up, and it was just at the angle Arim had hoped it would be. He still needed no binoculars to read the word he had printed in blue paint onto the yellow kite. COBRA.

Just as the line was beginning to run out, Arim realized that a man was coming toward him. The man was running. It was a race between the man and the line. The line ran off the spindle just as the man reached Arim.

"What the hell are you doing?" he cried.

111

Arim watched the line slipping away through the grass.

"Give me that!" said the man furiously. He was in Home Guard uniform.

Arim handed him the spindle. The man looked at it and realized that the line had run off it, and Arim saw that the line was now rising up into the air behind the kite.

The Home Guard man ran after the line and tried to catch it with his hands, as if chasing butterflies. Once or twice he almost succeeded, but then he stumbled and the end of the line vanished from Arim's view.

But he could see the kite. It was sailing on its way across the motorway, dead on course, aiming straight for the place where they had photographed the jeep with the rockets the day before. But because it had to carry the whole weight of the line now, it was losing height again. From where Arim was standing, it looked as if it were hovering just above the high tension wires with its long wet line dragging behind it.

28

Dan and Hanna were cycling as fast as they could toward Lundtofte. They rode through the gate into the forest, down toward the river, over the little bridge for cyclists and then hauled their bikes up the slope by the restaurant which stood by the motorway. They had been going so fast that they had no breath to talk. Dan looked at his watch when they got there. It was twelve minutes to eleven.

Where they were standing, they were a few meters from the motorway. They could see both bridges, and they could presumably be seen from both bridges, too.

No, thought Dan. I can see why they didn't put their jeep and rockets here. It'll be tricky managing Hanna's hopeless idea of a bike from here.

Hanna didn't look very optimistic about it either. She looked around the slope. Suddenly she dropped her bike and ran over to something that had caught her eye. Dan saw it, too, and ran after her.

It was a baby carriage, a broken wreck. But it still had all four wheels. Hanna and Dan looked quickly at each other and nodded.

It wasn't *quite* so hopeless as the idea with the bike, thought Dan. This could go all by itself.

When he looked back, he saw Arim's kite. It was on its way up and you could see something was written on it. You'd need binoculars to see that the word was "Cobra," but there would be some people who had.

Hanna had swiftly collected some bottles that were lying near the baby carriage and was putting them inside it. Dan watched her for a moment, and then joined her. They would fall out, if they were lucky, when the baby carriage toppled. They would be shattered, if they were even luckier. But they were going to need all that luck, Dan thought.

Together Dan and Hanna shoved the carriage full of empty bottles up onto a slight hummock. God knows what we look like in the binoculars of the police, thought Dan. A married couple with their baby? He looked at Hanna. She was slightly taller than him, but otherwise nice. She had hair the same color and curly just like he had.

They had reached the top of the slope and both of them were standing there with their hands holding the baby carriage. Arim's kite was on its way down again, Dan saw. But everyone would have seen it by now—whatever good that would do. Dan's heart was thumping and his mouth felt dry. He looked over toward Copenhagen and saw two helicopters and also glimpses of blue along the motorway. As he watched, the dots of blue were coming nearer.

As they got closer, he saw that they were police on motorbikes, and that they were trying to create a gap between themselves and the motorcade of black cars further back.

"Hello, you two!" a voice behind them shouted.

It was a man in Home Guard uniform. He was standing up by the restaurant, and he began to run down toward them, waving his arms.

Dan tried to calculate. In one minute, the man would have reached them. In two minutes, the first police motorcycles would pass down on the motorway. It couldn't be better. Sometimes, you were luckier than you deserved.

When the man was about twenty strides away from Dan and Hanna, they looked at each other and gave the baby carriage a hefty shove. The man saw it, stopped in confusion, started running, but now after the carriage. He ran faster than the baby carriage, which kept jerking to a stop, and Dan realized there was only one thing to do.

He ran straight across the man's course and aimed at his legs in a tackle that would have been a foul on the football field. The man fell and the revolver he had had in his hand went off.

The baby carriage rolled on, rapidly approaching the motorway. The man got up and began to run after the carriage again. It stopped.

Dan saw that Hanna had begun to run after the carriage, and that she had got a good head start on the man, but she couldn't run as fast as he could. I should have tackled him even harder, thought Dan. He got up and began to run.

Hanna reached the baby carriage first and gave it another shove. The Home Guard man got there the next moment, ran straight into Hanna, and they both fell. The baby carriage rolled peacefully out onto the motorway and stopped exactly where it should have. The next moment, two things happened.

Someone up on Lundtofte bridge lost his head and began to shoot. And a car which had been driving ahead of the police motorbikes hit the pram, tipped it over, and scattered a mass of broken glass before one of its tires exploded with a loud bang, which set off another salvo from up on the bridge.

The police motorbike collided with the punctured car and turned over, so that the whole road was blocked. The next police motorbike tried to steer around them, but the policeman fell off and the bike whizzed straight across the central strip of grass, turned over and caught fire. The Home Guard man rushed down toward the motorway, which was now totally blocked in both directions.

Dan walked calmly over to Hanna. They could do no more now, he thought. Things must take their course.

Frederik was cold.

His arms were bound behind his back and his legs were tied together at the ankles. He could do nothing to get warm.

The second dark-haired man came into view at the edge of the forest. He looked up before running across the short stretch between the edge of the forest to the clump of trees, and apparently caught sight of something, because he stopped, pointed upward and shouted something in English.

Frederik looked up. The object the man had seen was a yellow cross-kite. On the kite was written one word in large letters. To his astonishment, Frederik saw that the word was "Cobra."

The dark-haired man came running down to the two jeeps. He pointed again and shouted something.

"Cobra," he cried. "What's that? Who knows about us?"

The fair-haired man and the man in the mask looked up.

"Some kid flying a kite," said the fair-haired one.

"But it says *Cobra* on it," said the man in the mask.

"Get on with your jobs, for God's sake," shouted the fair-haired man.

The two dark men also shouted something and the fair man shouted back at them in English. The man in the mask couldn't take his eyes off the kite.

"It's coming down," he cried. "It's coming down toward us."

It was true. The kite was falling, as if there were no longer anyone holding the line. Frederik thought he recognized it. Wasn't it Arim's yellow kite? It'll land right here in a moment, he thought. But it didn't.

It landed on the high-tension wires, and at once the wires began to crackle and spark. Sparks ran right back along the line and over onto the other side of the motorway.

"Get on with it, for God's sake," cried the fair-haired man to the other three. He glanced up at the kite, which was making long sparks across the motorway and setting off a fireworks display just above them. He shook his head in amazement and then put his binoculars to his eyes again.

"They're coming," he cried. "I can see them. They're on their way toward the river bridge."

He repeated the message in English. The two dark-haired men and the man in the mask tore themselves away from the scene of the burning kite above their heads.

"Hurry, for God's sake," shouted the fair man to the other three. He glanced up at the kite again. At that moment, it snapped in half, half of it remaining across the high-tension wires, the other half falling not far from the clump of trees, and soon a large spark crackled through the rest of its line.

This made one of the two dark men react. He turned right around and fired a couple of shots at the burning kite, saw what it was he had shot at, and stood there slowly shaking his head.

At that moment Frederik heard a salvo of shots being fired

from the direction of Lundtofte, and a moment later another. "They've stopped!" cried the fair-haired man. "Someone's stopped them. Someone's shooting at them. A car has crashed. A motorcycle overturned. No, two motorcycles. One of them's on fire."

The next thing to happen was that another salvo of shots came from the bridge in Narum. The other half of the kite fell and Frederik reckoned that the shots must have been fired at the kite.

The fair-haired man stood tensely looking from one side to the other for a moment, toward Narum and then back toward Lundtofte. Then he relaxed and said calmly to the man in the mask:

"All right, that's it. Some other group has already got him. If . . ."

He smiled faintly.

"So we still have our lives ahead of us."

"Hostages?" asked the man in the mask.

The fair-haired man shook his head, smiling.

"Just get away quickly!"

The man in the mask shouted some orders in English. A moment later, the four men were in the jeep with the number plates and no rockets. The jeep started up and roared away.

Frederik fell over as the jeep drove away. He fell face down and for very good reasons could not get up again. As he lay there, looking at the last remains of a kite, presumably Arim's, and which had had "Cobra" on it, he heard the buzz of several helicopters on their way; he heard one single salvo of shots from somewhere; and he heard the stillness after the shots; and in the stillness he also heard the wind in the forest behind him, the forest he had known all his life, and that sound drowned the sound of a jeep in flight.

Frederik lay face down on the ground, thinking how good it was to be alive.

THREE MONTHS LATER

Dan was standing on the motorway bridge looking down at the cars.

It was one evening in May, and still light. Dan was going to see Arim and Hanna, and Frederik was coming, too, but Dan wanted to stand there for a moment first.

The last few months had been very confusing, and all four of them had had difficulty in what their parents called "getting back to normal." In March all four had gone through a period when school had been awful, they had been hostile both to their friends and to each other, and altogether they had a bad time. But that was all over now.

They had shaken hands with Henry Kreiser and had their pictures in the newspapers of the world. Kreiser had presented them each with a gold fountain pen that made blots.

They had visited the Queen and Prince Henrik. Prince Henrik had been so interested in what had happened to them that he had finally got them to draw a sketch map of where they had got the kite up, where they had pushed the baby carriage onto the motorway, and where Frederik had been hidden behind two jeeps.

They had been interviewed by journalists from all over the place, who had all put words that they hadn't said into their mouths as well as mixing up their names in the captions under the photographs.

They had all four said that they had been luckier than anyone deserved, but that hadn't been included. And Frederik had said that he should never have attempted to signal in Morse and that in fact he had run a fearful risk.

Now there was a man who was writing a book about the whole story. He seemed strangely absentminded when he asked them questions. No doubt he was going to elaborate enormously on the story.

One of the two policemen whose motorcycles had crashed had sprained his thumb, but no one else was injured, despite all the shooting by the police. But a week or two after the whole thing was over, Frederik's father had had a bad time and had to take a month off from work. He was all right again now.

Margrethe maintained now that she could remember it all. But when you pressed her, it was clear that she could hardly remember a single thing. She was very proud of the large doll she had been given, although, of course, she was far too old for dolls.

The four men who had lived for thirty-six hours in the Poulsens' house had not been captured, so they were still free. So was Henry Kreiser. And there was just as much rumpus all over the world as there always had been.

It was a lovely warm evening, the birds still singing, and down on the motorway a sports car came roaring along. Dan wasn't sure of the make. Then a police motorbike appeared with its flashing light on; another fine coming up, if the cops managed to collect it.

Dan stood with his bag in his hand. He lifted it up over the railing, which he did now and again.

When he joined Arim and Frederik and Hanna, there would be several words that were banned. If, for instance, you happened to say "*Cobra*" or "*Kreiser*," you had to put twenty-five ore in a box they had made. The box was already quite full, but now the number of twenty-five ores was not increasing so fast.

THREE MONTHS LATER

Actually, there were quite a lot of other things in the world to talk about.

A car drove under the bridge and Dan stood looking at his heavy bag, full of horror comics. He could let it go, or not. He didn't, and hauled it back over the railing again.

It's amazing, he thought, how many accidents you could cause, but which you didn't. On the whole, no one ever knew about the accidents people didn't cause.

He got onto his bike and rode swiftly off to join his friends.

MODERN

GYMNASTICS

TO RENEW THIS BOOK
CALL 275-5367

ARCO PUBLISHING, INC.
New York

Editor Mary Devine

Published 1985 by
Arco Publishing, Inc.
215 Park Avenue South,
New York, NY 10003

Library of Congress Cataloging in Publication Data

Aykroyd, Peter.
  Modern gymnastics.

  Rev. ed. of: Skills & tactics of gymnastics. c1980.
  includes index.
  1. Gymnastics.   I. Aykroyd, Peter.   Skills & tactics
of gymnastics.   II. Title.
GV461.A94   1985   796.4'1   84–24274

ISBN 0–668–06462–5

Printed and bound by Jerez Industrial S.A. Spain

CONTENTS

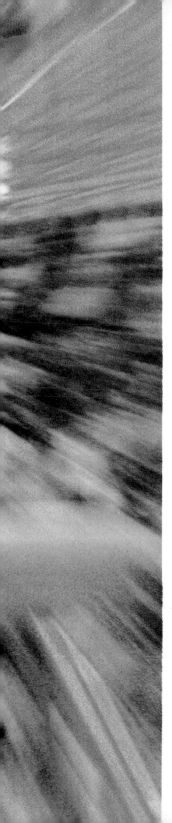

INTRODUCTION

To many gymnastics fans, the sport began in 1972. That was the year in which a teenage, gamine Soviet girl gymnast became one of the outstanding personalities of the Olympic Games in Munich. That girl was the unforgettable Olga Korbut. Her successes — and her failures — at Munich were seen by millions of viewers on television and a new era in sport had begun.

Olga captured the interest and imagination of young girls all over the world and the result was that gymnastics enjoyed a boom that has never been equalled by any other sport. Since 1972, the numbers of gymnasts and gymnastics clubs have increased at an incredible rate. For example, in the United States the number of competitive gymnasts grew tenfold over the following ten years. The United States Gymnastics Federation, the nation's governing body of gymnastics, estimates that America now has over seven million active women and girl gymnasts. The sport's international popularity today is boosted by nearly twenty million women and girl competitors in 81 countries across the world.

What did Olga Korbut do to attract so many young people to gymnastics? First, she showed that gymnastics was a sport that used the natural movements of lively youngsters. Most children at some time like to run, turn somersaults, perform cartwheels and so on. Second, Olga demonstrated that gymnastics has a frisson of danger about it. In other words, it was a sport that was more than just a collection of simple exercises. Finally, she made it clear that gymnastics has a strong element of art in its presentation because a gymnast — particularly a girl gymnast — has to express herself with grace and style. All these ingredients, together with the personality of Olga, captivated young girls in millions.

Olga, surprisingly enough, was never a world nor an Olympic champion. It took a Romanian girl to show the world the nearest to gymnastics perfection. Nadia Comaneci did not seem to bring the sense of enjoyment to gymnastics that Olga Korbut did but she brought technical brilliance that transformed all exercises. Nadia's first competition in the West was when she won the *Daily Mirror* Champions All in London in 1975. The virtually

Above: Nadia Comaneci of Romania proved to be the most technically perfect gymnast of the 1970s. She is the only gymnast to become European Champion three times in a row.

Right: When television brought Olga Korbut into the limelight at the 1972 Munich Olympic Games, gymnastics exploded into a boom sport.

unknown Romanian became a world star in the following year when she became Olympic champion in Montreal, achieving a perfect score — 10 — seven times. Before her retirement in 1984, Nadia was European champion three times, a record which still stands.

But gymnastics did not begin with Olga and Nadia. Its history can be traced back to ancient times and ancient civilizations — those of the Chinese, Indians, Persians, Greeks and Romans. The Greeks and Romans in particular set high store by physical culture but when their empires passed away, so did gymnastics in the form in which it was practised. It was up to acrobats and dancers for many successive centuries to perform movements similar to some parts of the sport as it is known today. For example, tumbling has passed down the ages as an entertainment.

In the eighteenth and nineteenth centuries, the importance of physical exercise began to attract the attention of educationalists in Denmark, Germany and Sweden and so once more, in various forms, gymnastics became popular. Physical fitness developed through

Below : Gymnastics has its roots in the games and sports of many past civilizations. This vase from Ancient Greece shows an acrobat performing.

Above: Balancing acts in many forms have long been popular entertainment, as this picture of the Forum in Ancient Rome demonstrates.

Right: There is a familiar look about the acrobatics portrayed in these seventeenth century German prints.

gymnastics was considered by many people to be vital in military training. A leading pioneer was Ludwig Jahn (1778-1839) of Germany who established many *turnverein* (gymnastics clubs) and developed such equipment as the rings, parallel bars, horizontal bar and the horse. The first gymnastics club in the United States was started in 1850, while the Amateur Gymnastics Association (now the British Amateur Gymnastics Association) was formed in 1888.

The enthusiasm for fitness in the nineteenth century, together with the growth of several sports, led to the founding of the first modern Olympic Games. These were held in Athens in 1896 and gymnastics was one of the seven sports included. It has been an Olympic sport ever since. Women's gymnastics were introduced to the Olympic Games in 1928 and subsequently developed into its four disciplines of vault, asymmetric bars, balance beam and floorwork which were much more suited to femininity than the strength pieces of men's gymnastics. Since 1952, women from the Soviet Union have dominated the Olympic Games. Among the most famous Soviet women stars of the last two decades have been Larissa Latynina and Ludmila Tourischeva. In 1968, however, a Czech gymnast, Vera Caslavska, won four gold medals at the Mexico Olympic Games.

Below: Ludmila Tourischeva of the Soviet Union was one of the great gymnasts of recent years. She achieved the top overall titles in the world – Olympic, World, World Cup and European. Ludmila is now a coach to a future generation of Soviet stars.

Above: The forerunner of the balance beam ? An eighteenth-century print from France shows tightrope walkers entertaining a crowd – but aided by balance poles.

Opposite (below): Gymnastics was included in the first post-War Olympic Games in London in 1948. It took the next Games, at Helsinki in 1952 when the Soviet Union participated for the first time, to shape women's gymnastics into its present form.

The International Federation of Gymnastics (FIG) was founded in 1881 with three member countries. Today, eighty-one countries belong to the FIG. Since 1950, the World Championships organized by the FIG, have been held every four years. From 1979, The World Championships take place in the year preceding the Olympic Games and is used as a qualifying tournament for the Games. In 1975 the World Cup was established and now takes place every four years. There are many important regional competitions, too, such as the Pan-American Games and European Championships.

Every member country of the FIG has a national federation which controls gymnastics through local member organizations. Most federations appoint national coaches who are responsible for keeping standards high and for selecting and training national teams. The basic unit in every federation is the school or neighbourhood gymnastics club from which every first-class gymnast starts on her career. The world-wide boom in gymnastics has meant, however, that in many countries there are too few coaches.

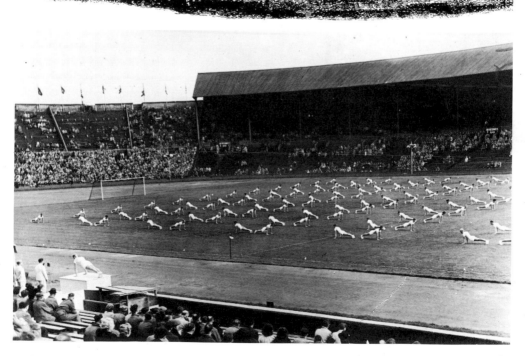

Most leading gymnasts have been encouraged in the sport at school. Gymnastics is now very popular with primary schools because it is not only a year-round activity but can also involve boys and girls. Basic gymnastics can be practised in assembly halls or gymnasiums and with equipment which many schools already have.

The greatest boost to modern gymnastics is undoubtedly television. The medium is ideal for the sport and is able to capture its visual qualities and project them to a world-wide audience. Television coverage of gymnastics on a universal scale began with the Olympic Games of 1960 in Rome, and since then, most of the world's most important gymnastics events have been televised and presented in some form to television audiences everywhere.

This book will tell you how to approach gymnastics if you are determined to reach the top. It does not offer you an easy formula for success. Nor can it explain and illustrate all the many moves that make up modern gymnastics. But it can introduce you to most of the elements you must master to become a competent gymnast. As with every other sport, to succeed you will need other qualities such as determination, good coaching and a great deal of natural ability.

If nothing else, this book will help you to understand something of an exciting sport which has moved from a minor position to a major place in physical culture in a few years. And, as you know, the more you understand it, the more you will enjoy it.

Opposite: Elena Davydova was one of many Soviet gymnasts who captivated world audiences. Here she is in 1978.

Below: Gymnastics owes its present popularity to television. A landmark was the first world-wide TV coverage of the sport at the 1960 Rome Olympic Games.

CHAPTER 1

PREPARING FOR GYMNASTICS

Thorough preparation is the key to success in gymnastics, not least because of the combination of different skills the sport requires.

How did you become interested in gymnastics? Many people's interest was aroused by watching some of the world's best gymnasts perform on television; gymnasts such as Olga Korbut, Olga Bicherova, Natalia Yurchenko, Mary Lou Retton and Julianne McNamara. Others may have been to a tournament, international match or display at which famous stars appeared. Wherever you have seen top-class gymnastics performed, you will, like millions of girls all over the world, have been attracted by the grace, skill and daring of the gymnasts.

Opposite: Some of the physical qualities required by a top gymnast.

You may already be a member of a gym club, either at one run at school or at one established in your home area. If so, you will know something of the ways by which gymnasts learn to master their sport. Like most keen gymnasts, you probably find that the training sessions at your club are lively and enjoyable. Most clubs have two sections: one for gymnasts who attend just for recreation, relaxation and enjoyment and the other for gymnasts with talent or who show signs of being able to become successful competitive gymnasts. If you belong to this second group of elite gymnasts and you, too, really want to succeed in gymnastics, there are four vital points which must be understood before serious training begins.

1. **It takes a long time to become a good gymnast.** Every star you see performing worked for years to get where she is. Thus gymnastics is a sport which requires endless patience and hard work.
2. **Gymnastics is a sport of individual performances.** In gymnastics, you are never seen to win a race or score points off an opponent. This means that you are not competing so much against other gymnasts as against yourself. The sweetest success for every gymnast is mastering the moves that must be learned to make progress.
3. **Your body must be in peak condition.** This goes for almost every sport but gymnastics makes particularly strenuous demands on the human frame. Therefore you must take good care of your body to achieve the best results.
4. **The best gymnasts are those who have learned gymnastics step by step.** When you are beginning gymnastics, it is very tempting to pay little attention to the basic skills and physical preparation and go for learning advanced moves and routines instead. The result will be that your exercises will receive low marks because you perform them without the finishing touches of style, mobility and expression. Remember the old saying: don't run before you can walk. To sum up, if you want to get to the top in gymnastics, you must spend time preparing your body and acquiring basic skills. Only then will you achieve success. But before you go into the gymnasium,

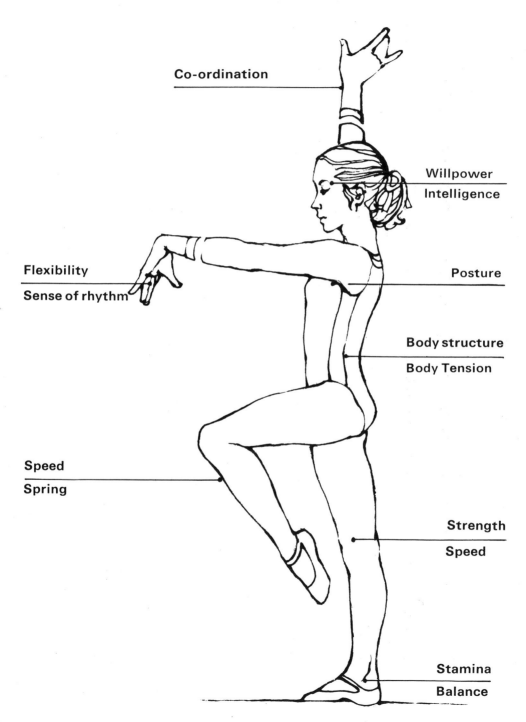

Co-ordination

Willpower

Intelligence

Flexibility

Sense of rhythm

Posture

Body structure

Body Tension

Speed

Spring

Strength

Speed

Stamina

Balance

19

you must learn about some factors that affect every gymnast. What makes a good gymnast? What raw material do leading coaches look for when they select girls for advanced training?

Ideally, gymnastics should be taken up between the ages of eight and ten. During this period, you should concentrate on learning basic skills. From ten to thirteen years, you will be linking these skills to form complete exercises and later you will be ready to learn the more difficult movements. As a matter of interest, scientists have found out that girls reach their greatest strength

Below: The career of the average gymnast starts when she is about eight years old and finishes when she is about 20. However, some gymnasts start as early as five years old and others are still competing well into their 20s

8–10   10–13   13–15   15–20

potential when they are between fifteen and nineteen years old. So in fact a talented gymnast can reach peak form at the age of fourteen to sixteen. As you may remember, Nadia Comaneci was fourteen when she won the overall title at the Montreal Olympic Games in 1976.

To become a good gymnast, then, you must have certain abilities which are part physical, part mental. Recently, some Soviet gymnastics experts made a list of qualities, in order of importance, required by the perfect gymnast. While very few people can call themselves 'ideal gymnasts', the list provides useful guidelines for any

Below: Nadia Comaneci became overall Olympic Champion when she was 14. This was at the 1976 Montreal Games.

gymnast who wants to understand what it means to aim for the top in gymnastics. The physical qualities, and many of them can be improved through exercises, are:

Strength. You must have strength throughout your body in the muscles of your arms, upper arms and wrists, legs, stomach, back and shoulders. Strength helps you perform your exercises without strain.

Stamina. You must be able to keep working without getting too tired. A top gymnast may have to train at least ten hours a week as well as taking part in competitions.

Co-ordination. This is a natural ability of combining movements of your limbs such as arms, trunk and legs. You will need this ability to link several skills together. You will also need a sense of timing.

Body structure. A gymnast of the right proportions will find it easier to make progress than one who lacks certain characteristics. For example, excess body weight will make harder work for your muscles. The ideal gymnast should have long fingers and arms with short legs and torso.

Flexibility. Suppleness in all joints — legs, back and particularly in the hip and shoulder regions — is essential to achieve the maximum possible range of movement.

Below and opposite: Some gymnasts find that they already possess essential physical qualities. Others may have to train hard to acquire them. All will have to combine them when learning movements.

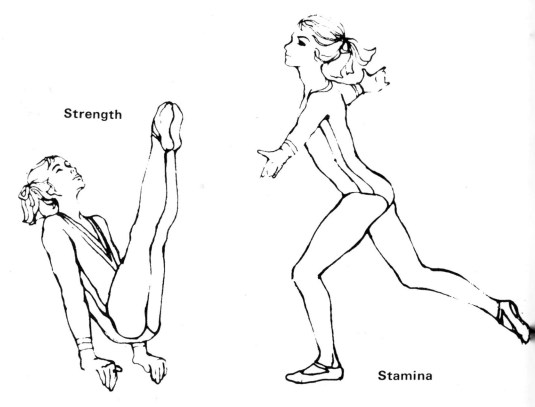

Strength

Stamina

Co-ordination

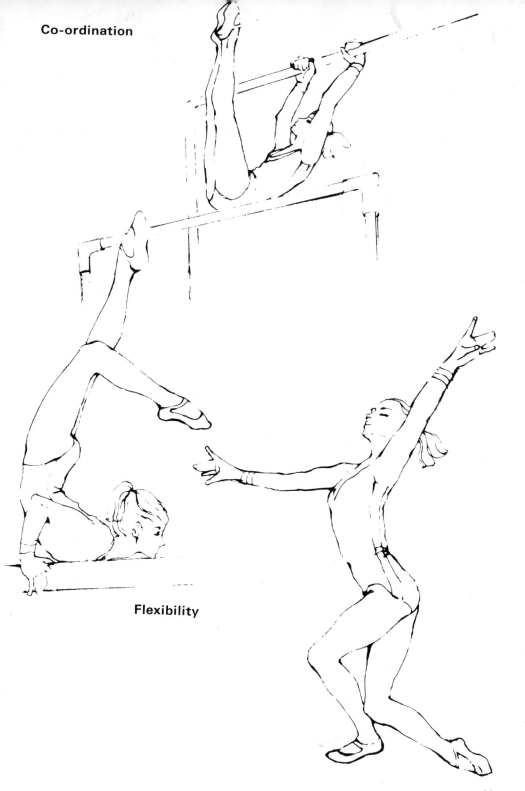

Flexibility

Spring

Balance

Speed

24

Spring. Being able to leap well is an essential part of many gymnastics movements. So your legs must have the power to lift you high.

Skill. Skill is part natural talent, part the ability to learn the essentials of a gymnastics movement very quickly and to perform it in the most confident way possible. Many famous gymnasts show this quality very early on in their gymnastics career.

Speed. A gymnast must be able to run quickly. This is essential for the vault and some tumbling moves.

Balance. No gymnast succeeds without ability to balance. Nowhere is this more apparent than on the balance beam where you have to perform on a platform not wider than four inches.

Sense of rhythm. You must, of course, be able to walk and run in time to music because floorwork is performed to music.

If these are the physical abilities which go towards making a top-class gymnast, what are the mental ones? Here they are, again in order of importance as the Soviet experts see them:

Opposite and below: The successful performance of difficult routines depends on mastering many skills requiring thorough physical preparation.

Willpower. Willpower covers determination, self-discipline, bravery and confidence. You may say that these qualities are connected. As we have seen, gymnastics calls for long, hard exhausting work, and for success, a gymnast must be prepared to undergo many pressures. A will to succeed, courage to tackle new and difficult skills and confidence in the outcome must go together with physical progress. As John Atkinson, Director of Coaching

Balance

Sense of rhythm

to the British Amateur Gymnastics Association, says: 'Talent alone is not enough when it comes to achieving really high standards.'

Intelligence. As a gymnast, you must be a clear, quick thinker, ready to co-operate in learning and mastering new moves and routines. You must also be able to adapt immediately to any mishaps in a routine during competition.

Expressiveness. Gymnastics, being a sport allied to art, has a creative element that calls for poise, imagination and elegance in its performance. A thoughtful gymnast will realize that, like a ballet dancer, she must convey mood and feeling to her audience by her movements. She must also show amplitude, a term meaning that every movement must be taken to its fullest and furthest point of stretch.

Emotional stability. A gymnast's life can be full of pain and frustration, triumphs and disappointments. You must have the self-discipline to come through times of stress without letting the occasions affect your temperament or your aim to be the best. Included here is the ability to accept strong criticism without getting upset and being able to work confidently without relying on encouragement too much.

If you belong to a gym club, you will obviously have many of these qualities. Others you can try to develop while you seek to improve your skills. But remember again that the way to the top in gymnastics depends on physical preparation combined with learning basic skills. That way, you will enjoy your sport even more.

Two other elements of a gymnast's make-up are:

Posture. An essential part of preparing for gymnastics is making sure that your posture is correct. You must know how to stand well and walk well. How well do you stand? Does your stomach stick out? Does your seat or do your knees stick out? Try and stand with your head held up and your shoulders back and relaxed and down. Keep your seat and stomach in and your feet straight. When you walk, try and do so with the same elegance and poise. Good posture not only creates a favourable impression with judges and audiences but also is necessary for balance and control throughout training and performances. Simple ballet exercises will help.

Body tension. A trained gymnast can control and tighten muscles in regions of her body so that they do not give way during an exercise. This is known as achieving body tension. The muscles most concerned are those in your stomach, back, seat and legs. You should practise tightening and relaxing these muscles as part of your training.

If preparing your body for gymnastics is vital, so is caring for your body. You must keep your skin clean; bacteria form if sweat is allowed to remain on your skin for long and this can produce sweat rash. So bathe or shower after a training session or competition and use soap. Take care of your hands; they are of fundamental importance in gymnastics. Keep them moist with hand lotion two or three times a day but never before practice. Nails should be kept short. It will help you to have hair that does not cover the eyes and which can be kept neat

Above: As well as being supple and strong, a gymnast must acquire a reliable sense of balance.

without too much attention. It must be tied back if you wear it long. Like all athletes, you should be aware of the value of getting a full night's sleep and of being a non-smoker. Do not train if you do not feel well, particularly if you feel feverish.

One important way for a gymnast to feel fitter and improve her performances is to know something about the food she eats and the science of nutrition. If you neglect your diet, your performance can be affected by deficiency in certain vitamins and minerals, lack of energy and weight problems. Good nutrition depends on your body having an adequate supply of nutrients, the components of food vital for health and well-being. Nutrients are classified as proteins, fats, carbohydrates, vitamins, minerals and water. As a gymnast, you will use a great deal of energy -- just the same as a footballer. The energy that food provides is measured by calories. According to Scilla Miller, an expert on nutrition, a girl weighing fifty kilos (110 lbs) will need about 2000 calories in a normal day. If she takes part in gymnastics for just one hour, she will need an additional 480 calories. If she has not eaten sufficient calories, she will have insufficient energy and will lose weight.

The main nutrients supplying energy are carbohydrates, proteins and fats, carbohydrates being the main source. Carbohydrates are the starches and sugars found in foods such as fruits, breads, vegetables, cakes and biscuits. Fats are plentiful in cheese, cream, butter, salad oils, bacon and nuts. Protein is supplied by meat, fish, milk, cheese, nuts and eggs and you should eat at least three of these foods a day. Protein is also the chief tissue builder and needed to repair and replace body tissue. Some nutritionists recommend that too much animal protein and fat should not be eaten.

In a good well-balanced diet, there should be no need for vitamin or mineral supplements but you should make sure of taking Vitamin C daily through fruits and salad foods. Otherwise, take multi-vitamin and mineral tablets. Drink plenty of liquids, too.

Some teenage girls feel tired, dizzy and have frequent headaches, leading to lower standards of performance. This could be deficiency in iron. Iron can be obtained from spinach, eggs, kidneys, liver and meat or in iron tablets prescribed by a doctor.

So do not let your eating habits hinder you from becoming a good gymnast. Two points to remember are: do not eat too much food or else you will clearly put on weight, and make sure that you always have a good breakfast. Research has shown that breakfast eaters are more alert and productive in the morning and more resistant to tiredness during the day than those who go without breakfast.

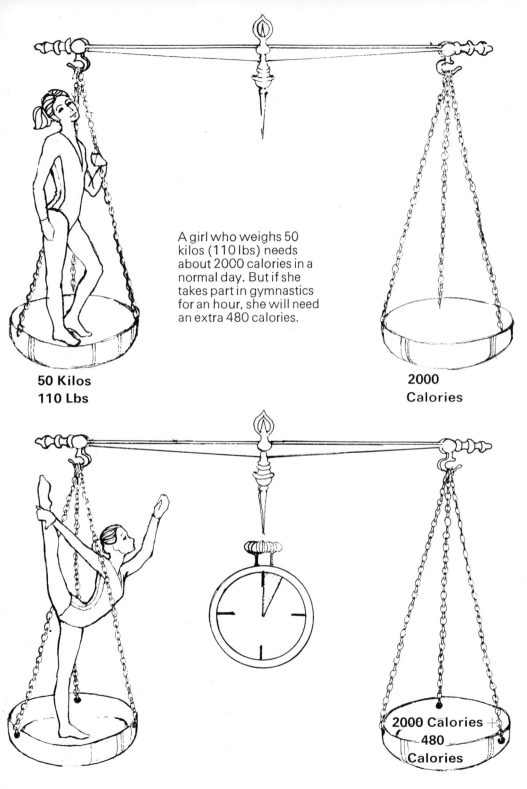

A girl who weighs 50 kilos (110 lbs) needs about 2000 calories in a normal day. But if she takes part in gymnastics for an hour, she will need an extra 480 calories.

50 Kilos
110 Lbs

2000
Calories

2000 Calories +
480
Calories

Keep-fit exercises for home

Exercising at home will not only keep you fit but also will help your physical preparation for gymnastics when you are not in a gymnasium. Here are some exercises which will help tone up all parts of your body. You need only spend a few minutes a day on them.

Running. Running is one of the simplest exercises of all. It uses most of your muscles and helps to give you stamina. Half a mile a day is ample.

Balance and posture. This exercise for the legs will help improve balance and posture. Just skip on the spot and raise your knees in turn as high as possible. Then see how long you can stand on the toes of one foot while holding the other knee up high.

Arms: swing. Stand with your feet slightly apart with your arms by your sides. Then raise your arms forward in line with your shoulders. Then, keeping them straight, swing them down and then up quickly in front of you to stretch above your head. Repeat several times.

Below: Daily exercises should involve every muscle. Strenous exercises however should not be undertaken until the body is warm.

Arms: strength. Lie on your stomach with your legs straight and toes pointed. Place your hands under your shoulders, press, and raise your body, keeping your knees and feet on the floor. Do this slowly. Lower your body and repeat before your chest touches the floor.

Shoulders. Standing straight with your feet apart, put your hands behind your seat with the palms together, keeping your arms straight. Then swing your arms sideways, still keeping them straight, to clap your hands high above your head. Then swing your arms down and clap them behind your seat. Repeat several times.

Stomach. Lie on your back with your arms stretched above your head. Raise each leg in turn off the floor to a height of 1 ft and hold for a short time. Then raise both legs together.

Waist. Stand with your feet apart. Reach over your head with your left arm towards your right side. Then slide your right arm down the side of your right leg as far as you can reach for six or seven times. Then repeat.

Below: There are many other exercises which you can perform. If you are in regular training, ask the advice of your coach, teacher or gymnastics club.

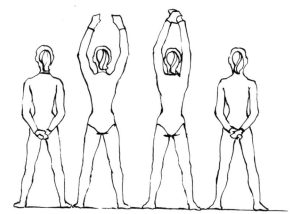

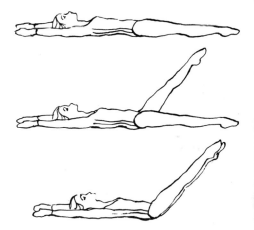

Body tension. Lie on the floor with your hands on a bench or side of a bed. Then, raise your body, keeping your feet on the floor. The aim is to get your body in a straight line from your hands to your feet.

Poise. Walk around with a book on your head. This will help you to stand and walk straight. There are other ways of learning about gymnastics at home too. Here are some ideas.

1. Become a member of your country's gymnastics federation. That way, you will learn about big national events and competitions.

2. Subscribe to gymnastics magazines. They provide up-to-date news as well as supplying interesting articles about training, gymnastics personalities and major international events.

3. Keep a scrapbook for useful pictures and newspaper clippings about gymnastics.

4. Get a notebook to write down any interesting facts that you may learn about the sport.

5. Try and watch top-class gymnastics. If you have the chance, go to any big event where advanced gymnastics is being performed. Or, look out for gymnastics events on television when they are presented by sports programmes.

6. Read books about gymnastics.

The next stage is to move into the gymnasium and see how you can tackle physical conditioning and learning essential skills.

Opposite: Elfie Schlegel of Canada won the overall title at the 1978 Commonwealth Games in Edmonton.

Below: See if you can persuade a friend or member of your family to exercise regularly with you.

CHAPTER 2

IN THE GYMNASIUM

Although gymnastics is a sport for individuals, a gymnast will spend most of her time in club training sessions in the gymnasium.

This section is for the conscientious gymnast who wants to do her best for herself and her club, and who has her sights set high.

Gym clubs today function in a great variety of places. Some are in modern sports centres. Others are in old converted buildings — sometimes even churches or warehouses. Many clubs are based in schools and others have to operate wherever they can find the space. Wherever your club is based, try and be a conscientious club member and co-operate as much as possible. Arrive for training and competitions on time. Help to take out and put away equipment. Be tidy in appearance and behaviour. Join in events that help to raise funds to buy equipment for the club, and always be prepared to learn about gymnastics from coaches and more experienced gymnasts.

It is through your club that you will receive the basic training to become a competent gymnast and that is why it is important to give as much to the club as you get out of it. The aim of this section is to give you hints to enable you to work at gymnastics in the club gym with as much confidence as possible. Some things will be obvious, others you will find are based on experience, and more will become apparent as progress is made. All of them will help make training more rewarding.

Clothing

For the most important items of dress, the club will probably have made some arrangement with a supplier. In general, though, all gymnastics clothing should fit well and be light. Some clubs allow their gymnasts to train in informal clothing such as sweaters and tights and here the same principle should be observed.

You should wear nothing loose that will get in the way as you perform movements, or anything dangerous such as buckle fasteners. All the clothing you wear for gymnastics should be kept clean, too, as this creates a favourable impression when you perform, and gives you confidence.

Track Suit. A track suit is a very good investment. Not only does it keep you warm but it also protects the skin from scrapes and abrasions during training. A well-fitting track suit can look very smart, too. Your club will probably have its own distinctive track suit which can be ordered when you join. Some clothing of this kind is necessary, particularly for warm-ups.

Leotard. As you will know, a leotard is essential for gymnastics. When you order this one-piece item, make sure that if fits really well. A leotard which is too tight or too loose-fitting looks most unattractive. At the same time, it must allow complete freedom of movement. Your club will have its own leotard for performances and displays and it is a good idea to order at least two so that you can have one spare.

Opposite: Track suits and leotards are clothing which every aspiring gymnast needs. Many clubs order them to their own design. Gymnasts should not practice on apparatus without adequate supervision.

36

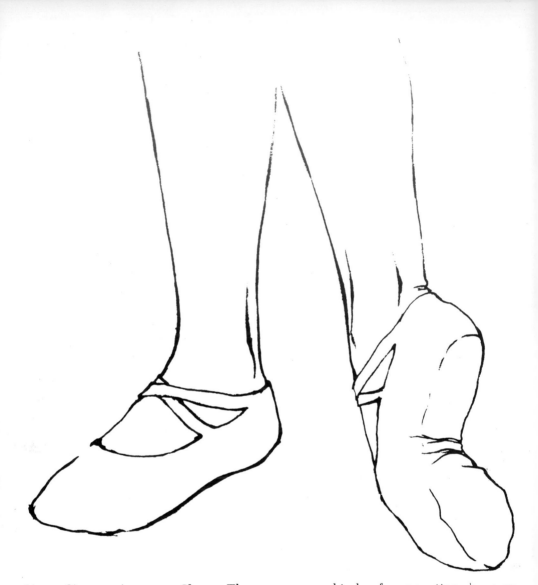

Above: Shoes and handguards must not only be comfortable but safe. They must never become worn nor slippery.

Shoes. There are many kinds of gymnastics shoes or slippers. These should be worn in preference to socks or bare feet when there is a risk of slipping or being injured. Socks should not be worn with slippers either, because they can make a gymnast look untidy. Gymnastics slippers should be light and fit securely, with light soles. Remember not to let the soles become too worn and slippery, or your slippers could let you down with a real, and very painful, bump.

Handguards. You will need a reliable pair of handguards for performing on the asymmetric bars. As their name implies, they guard the palms of the hands from friction caused as you swing on the bars. Handguards are made of leather, lamp wick or synthetic materials. They must

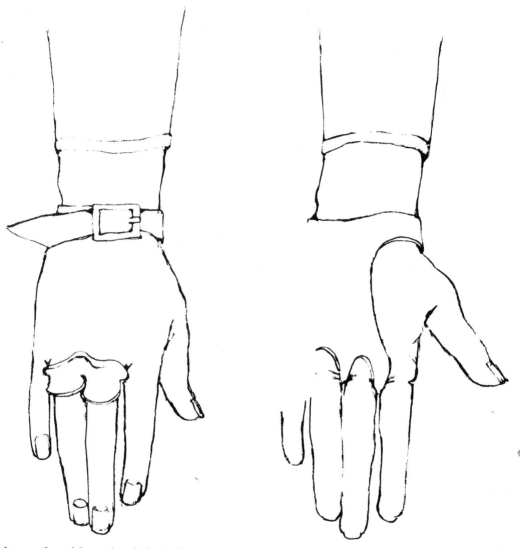

fit comfortably and tightly. When you try them on, place the two middle fingers in the holes and buckle the straps around your wrists. Because your hands have to grasp the bars, the handguards must fit snugly when the hands are cupped slightly. The smooth side of the handguards should lie on your palms so that the bars can be gripped with the rough side. It is important to check handguards regularly for wear. Make sure that the rough surface does not become too smooth so that your hands lose their grip. Do not use handguards if they are torn or if the stitching needs repair.

Hold-all. A very convenient item to have in the gym is a hold-all or duffle bag for your clothing and possessions. Try and obtain one which can be locked for security.

Learning aids

In your hold-all, keep a training notebook and pencil for recording any hints or training programmes given to you by your coach, or any good ideas that you come across during training sessions. Many gymnasts keep a spare music tape or cassette handy as this is useful for practising floor exercises. Another useful item to have in the gym is your own white, plastic-covered square tile, measuring, say, 150 × 150 × 1mm thick. On this square you can draw diagrams with felt tipped pens or magic markers and so use it to plot floor exercises. The diagrams can be changed or wiped off without difficulty.

Many gym clubs keep progress cards which show how their members are developing as gymnasts. You can do much the same by recording your own progress in a diary. You should write down each skill as you master it, and details of awards or achievements in training schemes or competitions. You will find it interesting, too, to make a note of when you train and for how long.

If you are fortunate, you may have a chance to see yourself performing on videotape. More and more clubs are investing in this playback medium because their members can then see and evaluate themselves when they tackle difficult moves. Coaches can stop the tape at any given point to show the gymnasts where execution needs correcting.

Below: A very useful item for gymnasts is a training notebook for recording tips, routines or other helpful ideas learned during training.

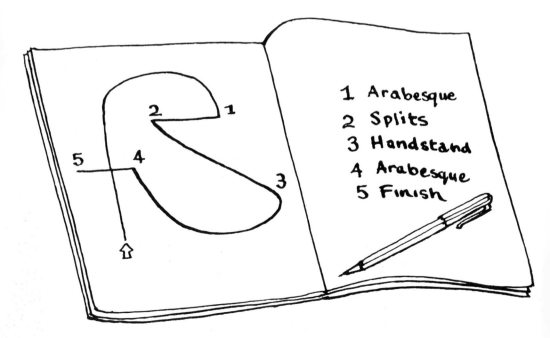

1 Arabesque
2 Splits
3 Handstand
4 Arabesque
5 Finish

Your coach

While you should always collect as much information as you can about gymnastics, you will learn most about your sport from your coach. In every club the number of coaches compared to the number of gymnasts varies: you may be coached as a member of a large group of gymnasts by just one coach. Really promising youngsters are sometimes able to have a coach all to themselves.

However you are coached, remember that the coach will be qualified and therefore have a great deal of experience in gymnastics. It is very much in your interest, therefore, to pay attention to and respect what your coach tells you. It may be a comment on a move, or an explanation of an exercise or an idea for a new element in a routine, but whatever it is you owe it to your coach to watch, listen and then experiment carefully. It is unfair on you, your fellow-gymnasts and your coach to waste time. A good coach will try and understand what kind of person as well as a gymnast you are so that he or she can help you perform your best in training or in competitions. This help will include drills, warm-up exercises and specific conditioning programmes for strength, flexibility and stamina.

Every gymnast should try and understand her coach. Do what he or she suggests and if you have any problems at all, speak up. You may have several coaches during your gymnastiscs career. Whoever they are, co-operate with them, because you cannot reach the top — and stay there — without their help.

Above: Romanian coach Bela Karoly not only discovered Nadia Comaneci when she was a little girl but also trained her into a world-class gymnast.
The influence of a coach can make all the difference to a gymnast's career.

The warm-up

A cardinal rule of gymnastics is that before starting any training or competition you must warm up your body. Serious accidents could occur if movements are tackled with 'cold' muscles, so the aim of the warm-up is to exercise all the joints so that the muscles are relaxed and stretched. At the end of the warm-up, specific exercises can be performed for suppling and strengthening. The body will warm up more quickly if warm clothing such as a sweater, track suit, or tights, is worn especially when you are training in a warm building. In its simplest form the warm-up period should last between twenty and thirty minutes. There are many suitable exercises for warming up and your coach or gym club will teach you some. Here are some suggestions of exercises for you to follow, in turn, which will warm you sufficiently at the start of a training session.

1. Start off gently by walking around the gym.
2. Then run on your toes, raising your knees.
3. Vary your running by skipping, side-stepping or making small leaps in the air.
4. Now stop running and exercise your shoulders. You

Below: Every gymnast must warm up for at least 20 minutes before training.

can do this by swinging your arms in different directions or circling them.

5. Then circle your hips — as with a hula hoop.

6. Sit, legs straight in front, and stretch the toes backwards and forwards.

7. Kneel and arch the body back. Then fling the arms up and backwards. Repeat.

8. Stretch your arms forward and above your head, hands back to back, fingers interlocked.

9. Stand and lunge quickly from side to side with your hands above your head.

After this, the body will be warm enough to try suppling exercises. Here are some examples of suppling exercises which will help you prepare for the harder skills in gymnastics.

1. Sit on the floor with legs straight and wide apart with toes pointed. Stretch forward with your arms and try and get your stomach on the floor (for legs and hips).

2. Sit with your legs straight in front of you and the back straight, too, and pull your body towards your toes (for hamstrings).

Below: Once your body is warmed up, you can move on to suppling exercises.

Above and opposite: It may take time to achieve the splits positions, but regular exercising will help.

3. Stand with your legs straight and together. Reach down, keeping your legs straight, to touch the floor beside your feet. Try and touch with your palms, hands facing backwards (for the hips).

4. Lie on your back with your knees bent and hands flat on the floor beside your head. Push up into a 'bridge' position (for shoulders and back).

5. Splits: with one leg bent and the other straight on the floor behind, bounce up and down. Increase the distance between your feet, ie move the front foot forward, until you move into the splits position. Then change around, with the other leg forward. For side splits, perform the same exercise with the legs astride. Your straight leg in either position must be kept stretched.

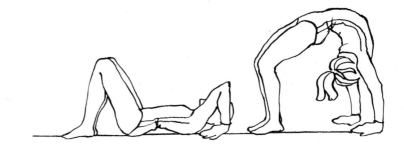

Training schemes and programmes

Can all the hard work which goes into training have an immediate purpose? Yes, it can. Most countries run national gymnastics programmes for girls at different levels. In the USA, the programmes are administered by the United States Gymnastics Federation (USGF), the governing body of the sport, and many of the organizations which belong to it such as the Association for Intercollegiate Women's Athletics and the National Association for Girls and Womens Sport. Each of the fifty states of the USA has a gymnastics association under which local clubs, schools and colleges can organise. Each year, millions of girls benefit directly from developmental and training programmes conducted by the USGF. These programmes lead to regional and national age group competitions at beginners', intermediate and advanced levels for girls from the age of nine upwards. Most of America's top girl gymnasts come from small independent clubs or schools which have excellent coaches, facilities and training programmes. If you, through your club or school, are involved in a national or, indeed, a regional training programme, make sure that you understand how the programme works. It is always more rewarding to train with a real objective in mind. Your club or your coach will help you decide when you are ready to enter an advanced training programme which may or may not end in a competition.

Safety

Because gymnastics has a strong element of danger in it, especially on apparatus such as the asymmetric bars, it is essential that everyone training or competing in the sport is aware of the need to observe safety rules. Safety is largely a matter of common sense; however, many gymnasts — even experienced ones — have to be reminded to be careful in the gym about grooming. Keep the following points in mind.

1. **Wear the right clothing.** Do not wear anything worn, loose or buckled which could get in the way of performance or interfere with the hands, feet or eyes.
2. **Do not wear jewellery.** Do not wear objects such as watches, bracelets, necklaces and so on. Glasses must be fastened securely.
3. **Check yourself.** Hair must never block the gymnast's vision. Tie it back if it is long. Also, make sure that the length of your nails does not interfere with your footing or grip.
4. **Keep your hands dry.** Gymnasts performing on the asymmetrical bars coat their hands in powder known as 'chalk' to keep their hands dry and therefore slippery. This powder is, in fact, magnesium carbonate which absorbs sweat efficiently. Dry hands generate less friction on the bars than sweaty ones.

There are other safety rules more specifically concerned with training. Your club should have a copy of the *Gymnastics Safety Manual* published by The Pennsylvania State University Press from which these rules are taken:

5. Do not fool around near gymnastics equipment.
6. Before using apparatus, make sure it is properly adjusted and secured with sufficient mats around it.
7. Do not use apparatus without qualified supervision.
8. Use proper warm-up and conditioning exercises before trying new and forceful moves.
9. Learn new skills in the right order. Check with your coach.
10. Do not attempt a new skill without a qualified instructor at hand
11. Learn how to dismount properly from apparatus before doing so. Ask your coach.
12. Any movement where you could land on your back or neck is dangerous and could cause serious injury.
13. Any activity involving motion, rotation or height could also cause serious injury.
14. Do not train or perform if you feel ill.

Below: A coach shows a gymnast the mixed grip on the bars.

First aid

This element of danger in gymnastics means that every now and then, someone is injured in the gym. Every gym club should have a comprehensive first aid kit and every gymnast should know where it is. Every club should also have someone qualified in first aid. If you are injured in the gym, tell your coach, even if the injury seems a small one, as treatment on the spot may mean quick recovery. If you have more than a minor injury, do not start training again until you have fully recovered. Many gymnasts have found to their cost that they have aggravated injuries by not allowing them a longer time to heal. Serious injuries will mean that the victim will have to go to hospital immediately. But for injuries which do not need hospital care at once, it is worthwhile knowing what to do in case there is no one qualified in first aid present at the time.

1. If there is bleeding, clean the area thoroughly. Then stop the bleeding by direct pressure and apply a sterile dressing.
2. Otherwise apply ice or freezer spray. If the ice is in a plastic bag, remember to place some cotton material between the bag and the skin.
3. Put a firm application of crepe bandage or elastic strapping around the injury.
4. Raise the affected limb as high as possible for 20 to 30 minutes. Remember, again, speedy and correct first aid is very important in the treatment of minor gymnastics injuries.

Bruised hips. A tip for girls whose hips get bruised while training on the asymmetric bars is to use vinyl foam under the leotard for protection.

Your hands. You should take special care with your hands as they are subjected to hard punishment when you work on the asymmetric bars. Keep them clean, well-conditioned, and protected with handguards. This will help prevent acute soreness: Do not let callouses become large; they can be ripped off with painful results and take a long time to heal. So trim callouses down with a pumice stone or emery board. If you get blisters, let the skin become hard before you remove it. After you have done so, keep the area moist with Vaseline to prevent it cracking.

If your hands feel very sore, give them a rest from the asymmetric bars and concentrate on other training.

Finally, treat every moment in the gymnasium as an opportunity to learn something about the sport. Remember, you can learn from your fellow gymnasts, too. Mistakes, new ideas, new achievements — all will contribute to your knowledge of a sport in which you must use your brain as well as your body to gain the greatest satisfaction.

Opposite: Elena Naimushina (USSR) 'chalks up' the asymmetric bars with magnesium carbonate powder. This will reduce 'drag' on her hands when she performs her routine.

CHAPTER 3

THE VAULT

At one time, it was thought that only male gymnasts could excel at vaulting. Today, that view is proved wrong at every major international competition.

It is particularly important to master the art of vaulting well, since it is the opening piece in women's gymnastics competition. The better you vault, the more confidence you will gain for performing on the other apparatus.

In a women's gymnastics competition, the vault is the first piece in the order of the four apparatus events. It is also the piece which takes the shortest time to perform, consisting as it does of a run, the actual vault, (during which the gymnast must place her hands on the horse) and a landing. In voluntary exercises, however, women are allowed two attempts at the vault — scoring with the better of the two — and this extends the time taken by each performer on the piece.

Many gymnasts tend to treat the vault as a simple exercise because it is so brief. This is a mistaken attitude because the vault is exactly the same in terms of value when marked as the other pieces are. So obviously a gymnast should make sure that her vault for a competition is the very best that she can perform. First competitions for young gymnasts are usually based on vaulting and floorwork and this is another reason why the vault should not be neglected in training. This is not to say that this movement is unpopular with gymnasts; on the contrary, it appeals to performers of all standards because it involves the excitement of speed, flight and daring. Gymnasts who execute a good vault at the beginning of a competition will be elated not only by their favourable start (and therefore good marks) but also by a sense of satisfaction.

What is the origin of vaulting in gymnastics? Historians are agreed that the horse — the item of equipment over which gymnasts vault — began with the dummy wooden horse used by Roman soldiers many centuries ago. The wooden horses helped Roman cavalrymen to learn the technique of mounting and dismounting from real horses. Later, knights of the Middle Ages who rode into battle wearing armour also trained on wooden horses. Thus the wooden horse was regarded for a long time as training equipment to mount or jump on.

When gymnastics began to develop as a modern sport in the nineteenth century, the wooden horse was already in use. It was usually covered with leather and sported a neck, saddle, croup, and pommel handles for basic swinging and circling exercises, the first of which were devised by Ludwig Jahn. Soon vaulting or jumping over the horse became another development of gymnastics technique and before long, vaulting became a standard exercise for physical education in many countries, Britain included. The horse then changed in appearance to the familiar leather-top box.

Both men and women vault in gymnastics; men with the horse placed lengthways (long horse) and women with the horse placed sideways (broad horse). For women, the horse must be adjusted to a height of 1m 20cm. The maximum width of the horse must be 1m 63cm. These measurements are laid down by the International

Gymnastics Federation (FIG). The run-up to the horse is made on a mat which is usually 24m in length. There are no rules about the actual length of run-up for women but leading coaches advise a minimum of 15m. An important item in vaulting is the springboard which helps the gymnast to gain elevation during the vault and can be used for mounting the asymmetric bars and beam as well. Specifications for the springboard are also drawn up by the FIG.

Below: The modern vaulting horse is the descendant of the dummy wooden horse on which Roman cavalrymen learned how to mount and dismount.

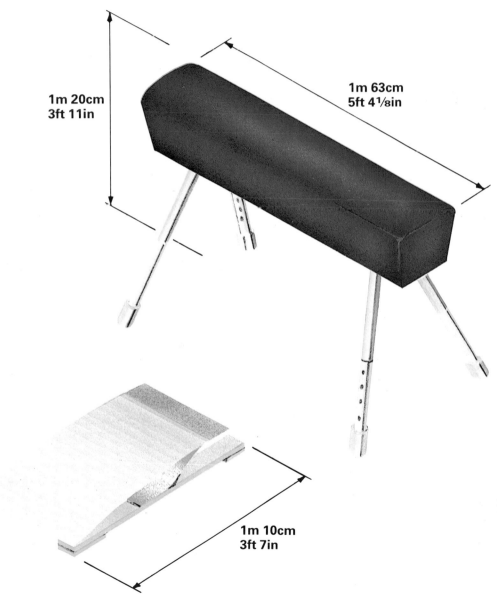

1m 20cm
3ft 11in

1m 63cm
5ft 4⅛in

1m 10cm
3ft 7in

Above: All vaults have six phases which follow each other in sequence. In them, except for the simplest vaults, the gymnast's body will turn on one of three axes, or a combination of more than one axis.

The rules governing competition vaulting and the three other gymnastics apparatus events are found in a book published by the FIG known as the *Code of Points*. As with the other apparatus pieces, vaulting is marked out of 10·00 points. Each vault has a rating which is found in the *Code of Points*. For example, a handspring vault will earn a gymnast a maximum of 9·40 points. Before her vault, if it is a voluntary one, the gymnast or her coach will indicate to the judges what vault she is going to perform. If her vault is very advanced and not in the *Code of Points*, a description of that vault has to be submitted to the authorities a month before the competition. In practice, however, only pioneering top gymnasts will perform advanced vaults other than the standard ones found in the *Code of Points*.

During the vault, points will be deducted for faults made by the gymnast. For example, bent legs can cost her up to 0·50 points as can insufficient height in her vault. The gymnast and her coach should be familiar with the general and specific faults which can lose her points. Interference by a coach once the gymnast has started her run can be penalized and could even make the vault void.

The marking for vaults in competitions is published in the *Code of Points*.

Analysis of a vault

When the human body turns, it rotates around an axis. Thus, in a cartwheel, the body turns on a front-back axis. In a spin, the rotation is around a vertical axis and in a somersault the body moves on a side axis.

In gymnastics, the simplest vaults feature no turns at all but as the gymnast progresses, she will learn vaults with a variety of turns in them. To sum up, vaults can be described as follows:

1. Straight vaults when the body does not turn at all.
2. Vaults around the side axis.
3. Vaults around the front-back axis.
4. Vaults around the vertical axis.
5. Vaults which combine turns around more than one body axis.

Whatever the vault, it will have six phases and each in its basic form must be understood by the gymnast. The phases are:

1. The run.
2. The take-off.
3. First flight.
4. Support position or thrust.
5. Second flight.
6. The landing.

Here is what the gymnast should aim to achieve during each phase:

The run. The gymnast must find a starting point for her run so that she reaches her maximum speed by the time of the take-off. She should measure her run so that she can start at the same distance from the horse wherever she competes. At the same time, she should count the number of paces in her run as this will help her timing on reaching the springboard. During the run itself, the gymnast will lean slightly forward with arms bent at the elbows, pumping backwards and forwards. She should run on her toes, increasing her speed.

In the last steps of the run, the gymnast will bring her arms quickly backwards before she jumps to land with both feet on the springboard prior to take-off. She must be careful not to slow her run at this point or make her last step too high. Before her feet touch the springboard, her arms must be swung forward quickly and upwards. Ideally, the upward motion of the arms will help depress the springboard thus giving the gymnast more power to her take-off.

The take-off. Legs and hips should be flexed slightly on the board with the body bent slightly at the hips. The more the body is bent at this stage, the more it will rotate, so for vaults which do not require considerable rotation the angle of lean should be slight. The push-up by the legs should not take place until the body's weight is ahead of the feet. The thrust of the legs should coincide with the upward stretch of the arms. So three forces must be used quickly to take the gymnast into first flight: the momentum of the run, the upwards stretch of the arms and the downward thrust of the legs.

Opposite: Two Natalias from the Soviet Union, Shaposhnikova and Yurchenko, prepare to begin their run-up to the horse.

The squat

First flight. This is the time between take-off and touching the horse. After take-off, the body will achieve maximum height with the feet moving to the rear. Factors affecting the movement of the feet in flight are the distance of the springboard from the horse and, as mentioned, how much the body is angled at take-off. For advanced vaults, the gymnast should develop a short, fast first flight. This will, of course, depend on the vault being attempted.

Support position. At this stage, the hands contact the horse parallel and flat with the fingers pointing in the direction of the vault. The hands must not be too wide apart. The shoulder joints should be flexed slightly and then stretched forcefully to give thrust upwards. This will maintain the body's lift.

Below: Speed, spring and thrust are the essentials of producing lift in a vault.

Straddle

Stoop

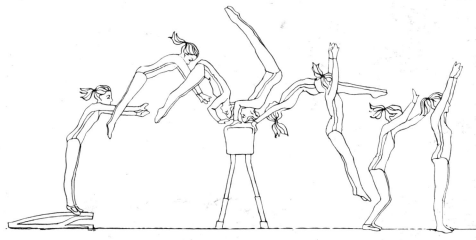

Headspring

Second flight. Each type of vault proceeds to the landing in a different way, with the body in varying positions or with actions such as twisting or somersaulting. Whatever vault the gymnast performs, she must end this phase with the body in a favourable position for a controlled landing.

The landing. In a perfect landing, the gymnast must stop on the ground without taking extra steps. Therefore she should arrive with her feet together and ahead of her body weight. Her knees should bend, but not too much, to absorb the horizontal pressure on her body to continue moving forwards. Her arms should be held up and back. Once landed, she should stand upright quickly.

Below: The landing is all-important for the gymnast. The more controlled it is, the better the impression made on judges and spectators.

Opposite: Elena Davydova executes a perfect landing.

Cartwheel

Hecht

60

Safety

Gymnasts practising vaulting should be aware of the need to observe safety measures, particularly around the approach area and landing zone. Gymnasts working on other training should be careful not to obstruct vaulters and they must be ready to warn anyone who might cause an obstruction. No one should vault without adequate supervision and safety mats available.

Training

Before tackling new vaults, the gymnast must have practised the basic skills of vaulting and, indeed, sought to have improved her standards. Some gymnasts are apprehensive about learning the vault; after all, to throw one's body into the air at speed over an obstacle can be daunting. But training that is carefully planned can instil confidence in the most timid of girls. From the beginning, it should be realized that gymnasts need not train with the horse at its full height of 1m 20cm as for competitions. The useful box horse found in so many gyms is thus invaluable for young gymnasts who can then practise their skills with the box set at any convenient height.

Initial training for vaulting should concentrate on the six phases of the vault as described above. It should be remembered that as the phases follow each other in sequence, the success of each part depends to a large extent on how the preceding one was executed. So, taking each phase in turn with the fundamental ones first, here are some approaches which can help improve performances.

Yamashita

The run. The run must be fast and efficient, with even paces. This can be developed by sprinting over short distances between 20m and 50m. If the gymnast finds it hard to keep her paces even, she can mark her run with lines. To start the run, rise on the toes and overbalance forwards.

Take-off. The gymnast should practise the step on to the springboard so that it does not become a hurdle to her, physically and mentally. Basic training here can be jumping from a bench on to the springboard and then off. As the gymnast improves, she can jump on to the board from a short run which she can lengthen while increasing her speed. Remember that the feet must land ahead of the hips with the arms held well back. As the arms come forward and up, ankles and knees push down to create lift off the springboard. A box horse or stacked crash mats placed at a low height beyond the springboard will give the gymnast incentive to strive for greater lift.

Landing. Landing is the third major part of vaulting and its practice should be incorporated in basic training. The gymnast can practise the landing from a low height using the box horse longways on and then increase the height. The jump down must avoid excessive arching of the back and the body should be tense in the air.

Below: Training for vaulting is very much a matter of acquiring confidence.

First flight. The aim is to increase the distance of flight between the springboard and horse. One method of training is to jump off the springboard and dive on to stacked crash mats, finishing with a forward roll. To encourage the gymnast to gain height, a low box horse can be placed between the springboard and the crash mats. The height of the horse can then be raised as the gymnast gains confidence. The vaulting horse can be substituted for the crash mats once the gymnast has acquired lift and height in her first flight.

Support position. Exercises here must help to strengthen the shoulders and wrists. An effective way is to swing the legs up as for a handstand but not raising them

Below: There are several ways in which aids can be used to help gymnasts learn the six phases of a vault.

Handspring

Tsukahara tucked

higher than 40°. Push strongly through the shoulders and either hop forward before placing the feet on the ground or push back on to the feet. A heavy weight such as a medicine ball can be held to the chest and thrust away as far as possible.

Second flight. Practice for the second flight, which ends in the landing, should ensure that the gymnast leaps high and covers as much distance as possible. As in training for the first flight, the gymnast can leap from the horse over a box horse with her body extended for the landing. A mark on the floor will give her a distance to aim for. Another exercise is to perform a handstand on the horse placed longways and then thrust with the arms, bringing the legs down to straddle the end of the horse before landing. This combines many elements of the vault but the gymnast will need support when trying it for the first time.

The vaults

As emphasized previously, the gymnast must master the simpler vaults before she attempts the more difficult ones. The group which follows is therefore of the basic kind and should be in every gymnast's 'repertoire'.

Basic vaults

The squat.
Straddle.
Stoop.
Headspring.
Squat with half turn.
Stoop with half turn.
Straddle with half turn.
Layout squat.
Layout straddle.
Layout stoop.
Cartwheel.
Handspring.

Now for vaults that call for more expertise. They should cause no great problem to the gymnast who learns her vaulting skills and movements thoroughly and progressively.

Advanced vaults

Cartwheel with quarter turn outward.
Hecht.
Yamashita.
Cartwheel with full turn outward.
Hecht with full turn.
Handspring with full turn.
Tsukahara tucked.
Tsukahara piked.
(Other advanced vaults may be taken from the *Code of Points.*)

Exercises to aid vaulting which can be undertaken at home.

These exercises, while particularly helpful to vaulters, can also form part of daily exercise routines.

1. Run on the spot with knees high, keeping on toes.
2. Skip with a rope.
3. Skip jump holding a weight to the chest.
4. Stand facing a wall and lean forward to support the body with one arm, the other held behind. Exchange arms, thrusting from the shoulder. Repeat rapidly.
5. Lie on your stomach with the thumbs linked behind the back. Bend the trunk backwards, so that the chest comes off the floor. Relax and repeat.

Gymnasts should set themselves a time limit for each exercise, say fifteen seconds, so that the performance of the exercise is balanced.

Finally, the keen gymnast will study the vaulting of other gymnasts so that she can recognise both faults and good points and relate them to her own experience. She should correct any defects in style that she might have at an early stage; otherwise they will be hard to change later on.

Opposite: Careful training on the vault is inevitably rewarded with good marks in competition.

Below: Keys to good elevation in vaulting are velocity from the run-up and thrust from arms and legs.

CHAPTER 4

THE FLOOR

The floor exercise is the
highspot of a competition
for the gymnast, and titles
are won or lost at this
stage.

The floor exercise in a women's gymnastics competition is the last one to be performed. It is usually welcomed with excitement for several reasons, and not only because it can be the climax to a closely-fought competition. In the first place, the floor exercise is a demonstration of natural movements. No equipment, apart from the mat on which the exercise is performed, is used to restrict the freedom of the gymnast. The basic movements of the floor exercise — and there are several — influence movements on the other apparatus. For example, the handstand and the somersault which gymnasts first learn on the floor, can be elements of moves performed on asymmetric bars, beam and vault.

Thus floorwork is the root of gymnastics and every gymnast learns skills on the floor as a first step. But the floor exercise is more than a collection of movements — it is a medium for the gymnast to express herself artistically. The big factor here is that the floor exercise is performed to music which links it firmly to art in the shape of dance. For just over a minute, the gymnast can project her personality through this combination of acrobatic skills and artistic expression to reach the imagination of her audience.

Show business? Perhaps in part, but floorwork is easily the most popular piece with audiences, and an exercise creatively performed will earn the gymnast her best applause of the competition.

Strangely enough, the floor exercise as we know it today is fairly new in gymnastics. It has its origins in the massed exercises staged in the nineteenth century in which hundreds of performers took part. There are still massed events at gymnastics festivals held in Europe, but these have very little connection with the modern floor exercise. As will be realized, massed displays have to be performed in large spaces, often outdoors, and when the modern Olympic Games were established in 1896, this pattern of gymnastic exercises was maintained. However, economy demanded in later Olympics that the number of performers, who were mostly men, were reduced. This in turn meant that the floor exercise lost the rigid formality which had previously been so necessary. By 1932 at the Los Angeles Olympic Games, men were performing an individual floor exercise for the first time. There are still massed events held at gymnastics festivals in Europe but these have no connection with the modern floor exercise.

For women, the individual floor exercise was included in a world competition for the first time at the World Championships of 1950. Six years later at the Melbourne Olympic Games, one of the greatest performers ever on the floor, Larissa Latynina of the Soviet Union won her first world gold medal on the piece. She was to win three other world medals for the floor exercise before she retired from international competition in 1965.

The modern floor exercise is performed on a square area 12m × 12m. For major competitions, the area consists of panels of elastically joined plywood layers on a rubber base. These layers are bonded by inserts with shock absorbent foam and covered with nylon carpet. The area is designed to absorb the shocks of the tumbling skills of the gymnasts, and is the only piece of equipment in gymnastics with exactly the same specifications for men and women.

Below: Mary Lou Retton captivated audiences at the 1984 Los Angeles Olympics with her exciting floor routine.

The women's floor exercise, then, is a combination of acrobatics, tumbling and dance. It should include leaps, turns, balances and poses. The gymnast must utilize the entire 12m square (but without going outside it) for no less than 1·10 minutes and not more than 1·30 minutes. As the *Code of Points* states: 'The clock will be started when the gymnast begins her exercise with a movement. It will stop when the gymnast remains in a stationary final pose. A signal will warn the gymnast at 1·25 minutes and a second time at 1·30 minutes. If the gymnast ends the exercise at the second signal, the exercise is considered to have corresponded to regulations.

The gymnast must link all movements together in a harmonious way that suits her personality and her build. The movements themselves should be balanced throughout the routine, and the whole must flow to a rhythm — and variations of it — according to the character of the music.

When planning her routine, the gymnast must pay heed to the requirements of the *Code of Points*. The routine must contain 'difficulties' which are movements found in the *Code*. These difficulties are either 'easy', 'medium' or 'superior' — A, B, or C — and the combination and number needed depends on the status of the competition. The routine must also include at least two groups of acrobatic movements and the final part should contain either a move or acrobatic combination of superior difficulty.

Opposite: Julianne McNamara is one of the United States' leading gymnasts. Here she is in the 1984 Los Angeles Olympics.

Below: Hayley Price, one of Britain's leading gymnasts, also took part in the 1984 Olympics.

How is the floor exercise marked? It is marked out of 10, in the same way as the asymmetric bars and beam are. Judges deduct points according to the faults committed by the gymnast.

In voluntary exercises, the points are distributed as follows:

Difficulty 3·00. For each missing superior C difficulty, the gymnast is penalized 0.60 points. Each B and A difficulty omitted will have 0·3 and 0·2 deducted respectively.

Bonus points 0·50. The gymnast can earn extra points for originality and risk in her routine, each factor being worth a maximum 0·20. A final bonus of 0·10 can be awarded for the additional inclusion of a C part, with or without risk.

Combination 2·50. This section includes parts which relate to the distribution of elements within the exercise, its composition, and the space, direction, tempo and rhythm used throughout the routine.

Execution and virtuosity 4·00. The execution of a routine — technique, amplitude, posture — can be worth 3·80 points, while virtuosity, or complete control, is set at 0·20.

In compulsory exercises, the gymnast has to perform according to the routine prepared for an actual competition. These exercises are also marked out of 10, with deductions as before for not including medium or

Below: The gymnast must understand what elements are required for her routine and how it is judged.

Handstand

Forward roll

74

superior difficulties and penalties of up to 0·2 for making small changes to the exercise.

General deductions. The gymnast can lose points for faults outside the classification of her performance. This list from the *Code of Points* gives some examples to keep in mind.

1. Failure to begin exercise within 30 seconds of official start: 0·50.
2. Fall on the floor: 0.50.
3. Support with two hands: 0·50.
4. Cross the boundary line with one or two feet or other parts of the body: each time 0·10.
5. Exercise without music: 0·50.
6. Exercise too long: 0·20.
7. Exercise too short: for each missing section 0·20.
8. Absence of acrobatic highpoints: 0·10.
9. Coach is present on the podium: 0·50.
10. Coach signals gymnast: 0·20.
11. Coach gives aid during exercise: 0·50.
12. Incorrect dress, missing starting number: for each violation 0·10.
13. Leaving the competition area without permission: 0·50.
14. Including elements of a 'theatrical' character: each 0·10.
15. Pauses longer than two seconds: each 0·10.
16. Moderate loss of balance: 0·30.

Below: As well as knowing how a floor exercise is judged, the gymnast must be aware of other ways she can forfeit points.

Handstand forward roll

Backward roll

Music. Ideally, the gymnast should have the services of a pianist available to accompany her during her floor exercise. A pianist can adapt, even compose a piece of music which can be tailored to fit the routine as well as reflect the personality of the gymnast. Whatever music is chosen, it must suit the movements or else the gymnast will lose points. The music can be orchestral or played by a piano or one other instrument. While the orchestral music must be recorded on tape, the piano accompaniment can be either on tape or live. So the gymnast must look out for music which appeals to her and which has variations of mood or rhythm around which a routine can be created. The music may have a brief introduction to give the gymnast a cue for starting her routine.

Check list

The following list will help the gymnast to construct the floor exercise routine which she can perform to her best ability.

1. The routine should emphasize the gymnast's strong points and play down skills which are poorly performed. For example, if the gymnast is particularly flexible in performing the splits, her routine should show this. Or, if she is very still in some limbs, the routine should avoid movements which emphasize this. Weak points must, however, be worked on for improvement during training.
2. Choose medium and superior difficulties which the gymnast can learn and use well. Select as many difficult actions as possible.
3. Find styles and moods of expression which suit the gymnast's personality. For example, an extrovert girl would need a livelier approach than a serious girl.
4. Make up some new movements for the routine. These could be steps or linkages, variations or combinations of movements.
5. Watch that the same element or position is not repeated exactly. An element can be repeated up to three times (with the exception of the back flip) if it is for an eye-catching purpose or to reflect a type of move. If an element is varied, started or finished differently, it is not considered a repetition.
6. Vary: speed and rhythm (which must match the music); body level; direction; distribution and combination of elements (which must link together smoothly); type of movement and body position (including arm and leg positions).
7. Use movements which you enjoy performing
8. Be aware of the general impression: posture, expression, presentation and so on.

Flexibility

When the gymnast has conscientiously and regularly carried out her suppling exercises as shown already on page 43, she will find her body becoming more and more flexible and ready to learn movements for the floor exercise and the other apparatus. Here are two more suppling exercises — to help side splits development and ankle suppleness. Remember that the body must be warmed up before undertaking any exercise that demands stretching of muscles.

1. Lie on the floor and place the seat and legs against a wall, legs pointing up. Open the legs and slide them down the wall as far as possible. Hold the legs in this position for a few minutes.

2. Kneel with the tips of the feet on the floor. Lean backwards so that the knees lift from the floor slightly. Again, hold this position for as long as possible.

Below: Once a gymnast is supple, she can tackle a variety of moves in the floor exercise.

Split position

Double bent-leg position

Yogi hand stand

Movements

These movements and positions will give the gymnast an excellent foundation from which to create her routines. The examples are given in the order of difficulty and the gymnast should try and master each one before going on to the next. Because these movements are essentially gymnastic and acrobatic, the gymnast must search for ways to express them as with dance movements, as part of a comprehensive floor routine.

Floor movements

Forward roll.
Backward roll.
Handstand.
Handstand forward roll.
Headspring.
Dive forward roll.
Forward walkover.
Cartwheel.
Round-off.
Backward roll to handstand.
Front handspring.

Below: Movements in a floor routine are performed in sequence, so the gymnast must devise natural links between them.

Forward walkover

Cartwheel

Tinsica.
Back flip.
Back walkover.
Valdez.
Front somersault.
Back somersault.
Aerial cartwheel.

Leaps
Split leap.
Stag leap.
Arch jump.

Stands
Arabesque.
Arched stand.
Scale backward.

Body waves
Body wave forward.
Body wave backward.
Body swing forward upward — to stage jump.
(Other movements and positions may be taken from the
Code of Points.)

Below: The experienced gymnast will always try to improve her floor routine – especially when she is competing regularly.

Round-off

Backward roll to handstand

Front handspring

Back flip

Above: Ballet exercises help the gymnast to improve the elegance of her movements in floor exercises.

Opposite: Ruth Adderley of the Ladywell Gymnastics Club was a British international in the early 1970s. Here she is in the middle of her floor exercise.

Ballet exercises

Because dance movements form such an important part of the floor exercise, leading gymnastics coaches are making sure that their gymnasts receive some form of ballet training. Ballet exercises are valuable in two ways. They help the gymnast to improve the elegance and poise of her body and they add strength to the back and legs. Ballet has three fundamental leg movements which contract and relax the muscles and which the gymnast can perform in the gymnasium or at home. They are: the *plié* (bending of the knees), the *relève* (rising to the ball of the foot) and the *battement tendu* (when the foot is stretched from a closed position to a pointed position on the floor). There are three positions of the feet from which to perform these exercises.

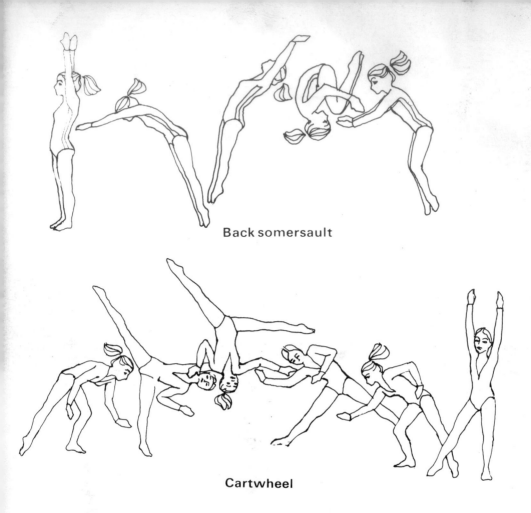

Back somersault

Cartwheel

Above: A sound training in ballet is essential for poise and grace in floor and beam exercises.

The gymnast should perform the following exercises holding a *barre*. This is the name given to the long railing at which ballet dancers train, but gymnasts can use the balance beam or the backs of chairs.

1. Face the *barre*, holding it lightly with both hands and with feet in first position. *Demi-plié* (bend knees, keeping heels on floor, straighten). *Relève* (rise to toes, lower heels). *Grand plié* (lower body until thighs are almost parallel to the floor and keeping body straight). *Relève* and repeat.

2. Repeat in second position. The heels should remain on the floor throughout *grand plié* in this position.

3. Repeat the first exercise but stand sideways to the *barre* holding with one hand and raising the other arm sideways to just below shoulder height in a gentle curve.

4. Repeat the second exercise standing sideways.

5. For the *battement tendu*, stand sideways to the *barre* with feet in the third position holding with one hand. Slide the outside foot forward along the floor until the heel has to be raised. Then arch the foot through the ball of the foot until the toes are pointed but still in contact with the floor. The leg must be turned out from the hip. Return the foot to the starting position and repeat to the side. Then repeat to the rear. On returning the foot, face the other way and repeat with the other foot. Careful performance of the *battement tendu* can strengthen the feet considerably.

The successful floor exercise has to be planned and practised again and again, but once the gymnast has found the routine which suits her and which stands out from those of her competitors, there is no greater thrill than performing to an appreciative audience.

Above: Ballet exercises can be performed in a class to music under the direction of a teacher or coach. Some clubs use the services of a dance teacher for ballet training.

CHAPTER 5

THE ASYMMETRIC BARS

The asymmetric bars is an exciting, punishing apparatus requiring strength and concentration, and including an element of danger. Do not, however, be daunted by the asymmetric bars – simply treat them with respect.

Asymmetric bars, high-and-low bars, uneven parallel bars — there are several names for this exciting piece of apparatus in women's gymnastics. But whatever gymnasts call the bars, they are all agreed on one fact: the asymmetric bars is the hardest piece of the four apparatus to learn. Why should this be?

The bars require strength, speed, suppleness, balance and timing; qualities which cannot be developed without considerable training. The asymmetric bars, too, is a punishing exercise, causing bruised thighs where the gymnast hits the equipment at speed and calloused hands from swinging on the bars. The difficulty of the piece is further complicated in that the bars present the gymnast with a very wide range of skills to master. This also means that leading international gymnasts are continually producing new and thrilling movements on the bars.

The asymmetric bars are a variation of the parallel bars used by male gymnasts and which were developed in the nineteenth century by Ludwig Jahn, the father of gymnastics. Jahn only evolved the parallel bars because he needed a piece of equipment to help young German men improve their work on the pommelled horse. The parallel bars were thus designed to enable gymnasts to gain arm and shoulder strength.

Until the 1930s, women used the parallel bars for exercise but it became clear that the piece demanded such strength that it was unsuitable for women. As a result, modifications were made to the parallel bars so that one bar was almost a metre below the other. This new equipment was demonstrated at the 1936 Olympic Games in Berlin and was used for the first time in the Games at Helsinki in 1952. Since then, the skills on the asymmetric bars have developed along the lines of those performed on the men's horizontal bar and consist mostly of swinging and circling movements.

The modern apparatus, then, consists of two bars, each 3·5m long. The high bar is set at 2·3m from the ground and the low bar, which is flush with the high bar, is at a height of 1·5m. The gymnast may widen or narrow the horizontal distance between the bars to suit her height and reach by means of two handles. The maximum distance the bars may be apart is ·78m and the minimum ·43m. Each bar must be 4·2cm in width and 4·8cm in height. As mentioned previously, for certain movements when the gymnast mounts the bars, she can leap from a springboard which is used for vaulting. In competition, the asymmetric bars is the second piece of apparatus, following the vault.

Apart from swinging movements, which dominate, an asymmetric bars' routine must include bar changes (the gymnast has to move to, and perform on, each bar frequently), changes of support positions on the bars,

Opposite: The specification for the asymmetric bars is published in the *Code of Points.* The gymnast can alter the distance between the bars to suit her height and reach.

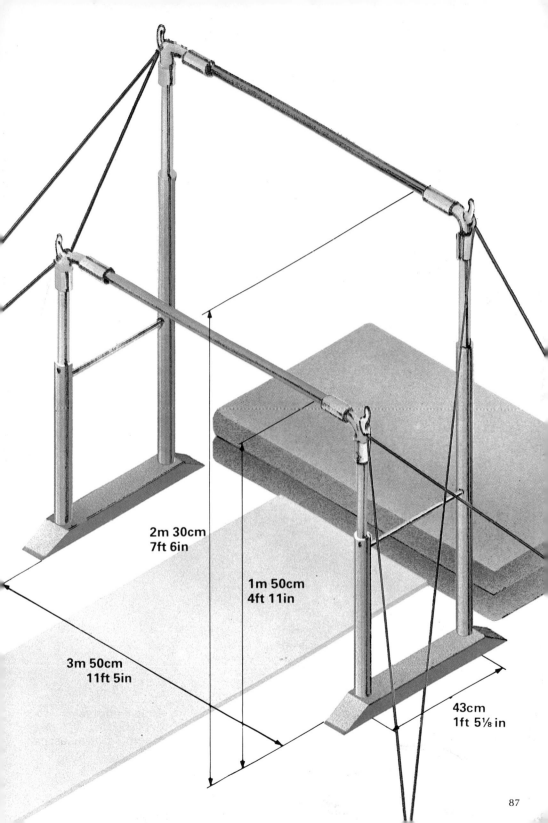

2m 30cm
7ft 6in

1m 50cm
4ft 11in

3m 50cm
11ft 5in

43cm
1ft 5⅛ in

87

and changes in direction of movement, all without stops or pauses. The gymnast may dismount (land) only from swinging movements and not from a stationary position. She is allowed thirty seconds to remount the bars. If she fails to do so, her routine is judged to be completed. She is also allowed a run for her mount but must not run under the bars or touch them. As with the floor and beam exercises, a bars routine must include a combination of difficulties from the *Code of Points* — superior, medium and easy. The gymnast is marked in the same way as in the floor exercise.

General deductions. Points may be deducted from the gymnast's score on the asymmetric bars if she or her coach commit the following faults:

1. Fall on the floor or apparatus: 0·50.
2. Touching the floor: up to 0·30.
3. Intermediate swing (swing from knees): 0·30.
4. Stop in the exercise: each time 0·10.
5. Assistance during exercise (coach touches gymnast): 0·50.
6. Assistance during dismount: 0·50.

Below: Olga Korbut was an accomplished performer on the asymmetric bars. She won silver medals for this apparatus at the 1972 Olympic Games and the 1974 World Championships.

7. Dismount not corresponding to the required difficulty level: 0·20.

8. Inadequate spacing and timing in progress of difficulties: up to 0·20.

9. Exercise not composed from required element groups: up to 0·20.

10. Monotony in presentation: up to 0·20.

11. Execution mostly in one direction: up to 0·20.

12. Exercise contains uncharacteristic elements: up to 0·20.

13. Monotony in rhythm: up to 0·20.

14. Too short an exercise (less than ten elements): 0·20.

Below: Most gymnasts check the asymmetric bars before their routine for adjustment.

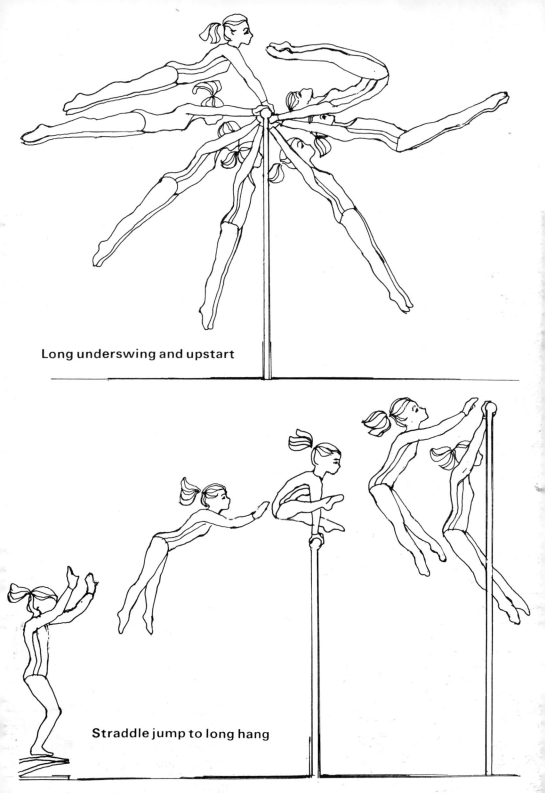

Long underswing and upstart

Straddle jump to long hang

Above: A gymnast's hands are most important to her for bar work. She must make sure that they are cared for ; otherwise the asymmetric bars could be damaging and painful to them.

Training

In training for the asymmetric bars, the gymnast must take care of her hands. As indicated before, she must use hand lotion to help protect the skin of her palms, she must wear handguards from the start, and she should 'chalk' her hands before she works on the bars.

Her body preparation must aim to improve the strength of her arms, shoulders and stomach area and she should carry out exercises for this purpose. Some examples have been given on page 44 and more are shown at the end of this section. The gymnast should also aim to become supple in the hips.

Many asymmetric bars skills can be learned on a single bar and, if it will give the gymnast more confidence during early stages, the bar can be set lower than the official height. Plenty of mats should be used around

the bars to cushion falls, and a coach or qualified teacher should supervise all training.

We have seen how the box horse and stacked crash mats set at different heights can be useful in training for the vault. In the same way, these items of equipment can be very helpful when the gymnast is tentatively practising moves for the first time. An unconventional aid used with great success by former British national coach Pauline Prestidge is the humble broom handle held horizontally to recreate the position of the lower bar. This can help the gymnast become familiar with certain positions. Some gym clubs, especially new ones, may not have the use of a full set of asymmetric bars, but this should not stop their gymnasts from preparing themselves for work on the bars.

There are four grips on the bars with which the

Above: To guard against bruising while training, the bars can be padded with foam.

Opposite: This gymnast is demonstrating front support on the high bar. Front support is a basic position in bar work and is used on the beam as well.

gymnast must familiarize herself. The three most commonly used ones are regular grip, reverse grip and mixed grip. The fourth, used more as a 'catch' than a grip is dislocation.

The gymnast must use the right grip for the movement she is performing. The basic support positions on the bar all employ the regular grip. The positions are: front support, back support, mill support, long hang and piked hang.

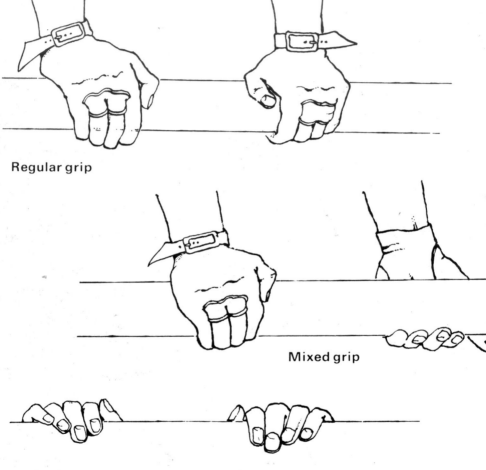

Regular grip

Mixed grip

Reverse grip

Above: Early training on the asymmetric bars should include swinging practice. This will help the gymnast to strengthen her grip and give her confidence.

A basic movement on the asymmetric bars is swinging, and the gymnast should spend some time getting used to swinging backwards and forwards in long hang on the practice bar. Swinging practice helps to develop grip strength as well as self confidence. The hands should be in regular grip and the arms straight, and the gymnast must keep her body straight as she swings. She must also aim to swing her body up to an almost horizontal position. At the end of the backward swings, she should try and release her hands and grasp the bar again before swinging forward once more.

When she can swing smoothly and easily, the gymnast should try making half-turns when her body is approaching the horizontal. This is performed by

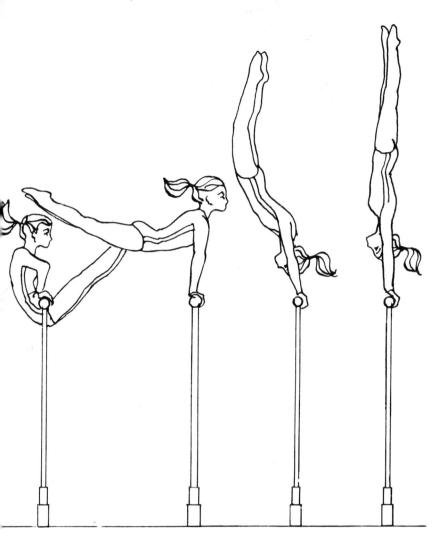

releasing one hand and turning towards the hand still grasping the bar. After this half-turn, the bar is grasped again, with the hands in mixed grip. At the end of the rear swing, the hands can let go to grasp in regular grip again. Half turns can be made at the end of alternate swings but remember that releasing each hand in turn will cause the gymnast to 'travel' along the bar.

An important 'swing' is the underswing which forms part of many movements on the bars. This is achieved by the gymnast holding the bar at arm's length in regular grip and jumping back and up, thus gaining height before swinging forwards, to stretch the legs straight out in front. In fact, the whole body should be extended at the end of the swing forward.

Above: Swinging practice should include half-turns and underswings as these can be used in routines.

From swinging, the gymnast progresses to circling the bar. Hip circles, for example, can be performed forward or backward from front support. In the backward hip circle, the gymnast swings her legs first forward then back so that she is horizontal, with her shoulders over the bar and her arms straight. On the return forward swing, her hips come to the bar and her shoulders drop back for the circle round the bar to return to front support. In the forward hip circle, the gymnast falls forward with her body slightly piked or bent forward from the waist. Her hands should move under the bar ahead of the gymnast to be ready to help swing back to front support. The bar must be kept close to the hips.

Another circle to practise is the mill circle from mill support, which may also be performed forwards or backwards. In forward hip and mill circles, the gymnast can reach out to catch the high bar if the movement is being performed on the low one. This can be done when the gymnast is facing outwards (away from the high bar)

Long hang on high bar, kip up to front support

and when she is approaching the upright position again.

Further circles to master are the seat circles — forward and backward — and sole circles. The seat circles are commenced in the back support position. For the back seat circle, the gymnast lifts her legs to the piked position, hands in regular grip. She then drops back and circles the bar to return to the back support position. In the front seat circle, the gymnast's hands must be in reverse grip. She falls forward to a piked position from which she unfolds as she swings around to the back support position again.

Sole circles on the low bar lead on to other movements such as catching the high bar or dismounting. They are performed in the straddle or stoop position with the feet on the bar, and the gymnast can circle forward or backward. As with other movements on the asymmetric bars, sole circles must be regarded as elements of one smooth continuous routine.

The gymnast must be accustomed to straddle or squat

Dislocation catch

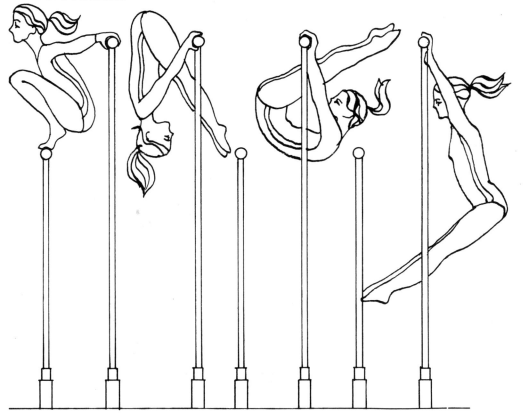

Above: The gymnast should only learn new positions or movements with the help of a qualified coach or teacher.

on the bars as these, too, are basic parts of other movements. The handstand, an element used on all four pieces of apparatus, should be practised as well. To repeat: new positions or movements must be learned with the aid and support of a qualified coach or teacher.

Once basic skills have been practised and learned

comprehensively, the gymnast can increase her repertoire by tackling more advanced moves. These can be placed into the following groups: mounts, upward swings and circles, kips (A kip is when the body is raised from a hang position to a support one), handstands, pirouettes, somersaults and dismounts.

Above: When the gymnast has acquired confidence by learning basic skills, she can begin to practise more advanced moves.

The following are examples of well-known advanced moves which can be seen in top competitions.

Mounts

Long underswing and upstart.

Straddle jump to long hang.

Free jump to front support on high bar.

Free jump with ½ turn to long hang.

Free jump with ½ turn to front support on high bar.

Jump to front support, hip circle to handstand.

Upward swings and circles

Free jump to front support on high bar.

Upstart from low bar to high bar.

Long swing and backward hip circle.

Dislocation catch.

Rear support to rear support on high bar.

Rear lying hang, stoop through, kip to rear support.

Kips

Long hang on high bar, kip up to front support.

Below: A routine on the asymmetric bars has to be planned so that the movements flow naturally after each other.

Hecht dismount

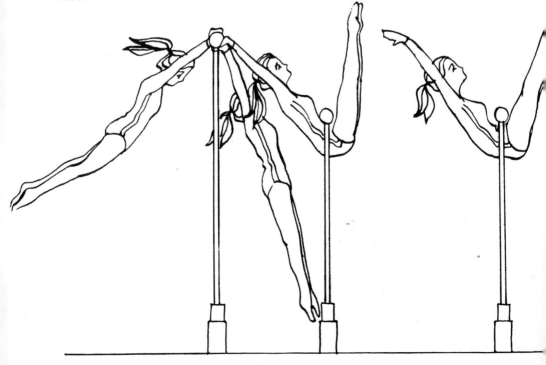

Outer rear support, ¾ seat circle.

Glide kip with ½ turn to rear support on low bar. A pirouette movement.

Handstands

Handstand from low bar to high bar.

Front support, hip circle to handstand.

Somersaults

Korbut.

Radochla.

Squat stand on low bar to back somersault tucked to catch high bar.

Janz roll.

Dismounts

Underswing dismount.

Handstand dismount.

Hecht dismount.

Jump to handstand, straddle or stoop off.

Stoop on high bar, forward somersault off.

Above: The handstand, which is a basic floor skill, can be incorporated into routines on the asymmetric bars.

Opposite: From front support, the gymnast can circle the bar to front support again.

To sum up, the asymmetric bars require many skills from the gymnast and these must be learned progressively. Only by learning them carefully, can the gymnast hope to become a competent performer on this difficult apparatus. The asymmetric bars also demand bravery in the execution of certain spectacular moves and this is another good reason to tackle the bars at a sure and steady pace. Once the bars are mastered, however, the gymnast will enjoy the challenge of risk, speed and timing.

CHAPTER 6

THE BALANCE BEAM

To the uninitiated, performing on the beam looks simple. In reality, however, it requires superb balance and concentration. Once a young gymnast has mastered the basic skills involved in a beam routine, she will have made great progress towards becoming a first-class gymnast.

To the spectator, a performance on the balance beam seems the most leisurely of all gymnastics exercises. The gymnast gives the impression of taking her time; nowhere in her routine is there a place for speed as there is on the other three apparatus. No wonder the beam is beloved of photographers, because this serenity which is so much a feature of beam work can be captured by the camera without much difficulty. However, the role of the beam has changed in recent times so that it is now much more than a means for women to demonstrate simple balances. It is true to say that almost any tumbling skill which is performed on the floor can be executed by top gymnasts on the beam.

The Swedish pioneer Pehr Henrik Ling used a version of the beam in the mid-nineteenth century. Apart from

Below: In recent years, a major improvement was made to the beam by the addition of a chamois leather-type covering which makes the surface less slippery and therefore safer for the gymnast.

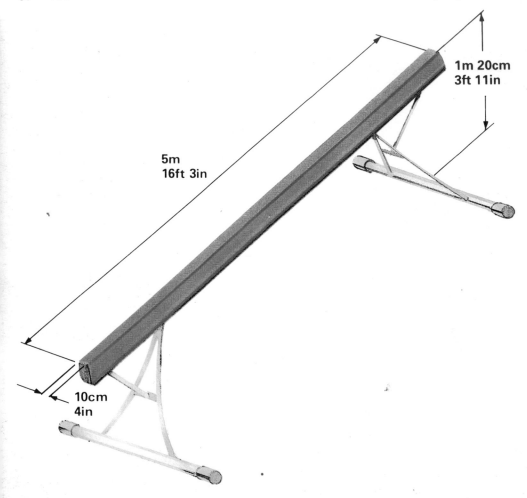

1m 20cm
3ft 11in

5m
16ft 3in

10cm
4in

developing a sense of balance, the beam was used to encourage good posture, co-ordination and grace. The apparatus was unique in that it was designed exclusively with women in mind. There is no equivalent of the beam in men's gymnastics. The greatest advance in beam technique has been, as could be expected, during the last twenty-five years. The world's top gymnasts today show what a versatile piece the beam is by the range of movement which can be performed on it.

But balance is still the key to successful performing on the beam. The gymnast has to perform on a long, narrow platform which is 5m long and only 10cm wide. What is more, the beam is 1·2m high off the ground and thus the young gymnast can be forgiven if at first she finds the idea of performing on the beam daunting.

Below: Svetlana Agapova of the Soviet Union is about to perform a Valdez move on the beam. This means that she will move backwards to a handstand position.

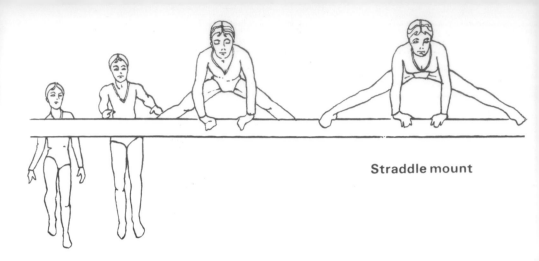

Straddle mount

Above: When a gymnast and her coach compose a beam routine, they must follow the regulations laid down in the *Code of Points*.

Let us see what the beam exercise requires of the gymnast.

Composition. The beam exercise is essentially one of balance composed of acrobatic and gymnastics movements. According to the *Code of Points*, the exercise should contain elements of balance, turns and pivots (one being a 360° turn moving forward, backward or sideways), leaps, jumps and hops (one of these must be a large one), steps and running combinations, acrobatic parts and connections, and elements close to the beam and above the beam.

The gymnast's routine must also keep to these rules:

1. There must be harmonious and dynamic change between the groups of movements.
2. The gymnast must avoid any repetition of movements but if she does repeat an element, she must perform it with a different connection or linkage.
3. Difficulties must be spread throughout the entire exercise.
4. The gymnast must use the whole length of the beam.
5. The mount and dismount must be in harmony to the difficulty of the exercise.
6. The gymnast should try not to use too many sitting and lying positions.

Rhythm. While the rhythm of the exercise must vary from lively to slow it must always flow smoothly without interruption. The gymnast should be careful not to perform an exercise that is not only slow and monotonous but also punctuated with pauses. Three stops are, however, permitted during the exercise:

Squat on mount

1. After planned, technically good and consciously held positions.
2. After any acrobatic stand such as the headstand or shoulder stand.
3. After gymnastic stands with held positions at the end of tho movement.

Pauses before and after acrobatic elements can be penalized by 0·20 points each.

Duration. The time limit of the beam exercise is between 1·10 min and 1·30 min. Timekeeping starts when the gymnast's feet have left the floor or springboard and finishes when they touch the floor again as she finishes the routine. A signal warns the gymnast when she reaches 1·25 min and again when she comes up to 1·30. If she has dismounted at the second signal, her dismount and the duration of the exercise will be regarded as corresponding to the rules. The *Code of Points* further states that all elements executed after 1·30 minutes will not be evaluated. If the required difficulties have not been executed during the 1·30 minutes, an additional deduction of 0·30 points or 0·60 points will be made for each, depending on the value of the difficulty.

Falls. Rarely does a competition pass without a gymnast falling from the beam. If a gymnast falls, she will be penalized as indicated overleaf. She may, however, continue the exercise, if she remounts within 10 seconds. If she fails to remount after the 10 seconds are up, the exercise is considered to have ended.

Approach. The gymnast is allowed one additional approach run if she has not touched the beam on her first.

Above: Outside her actual performance on the beam, the gymnast can be penalized for such faults as exceeding the time limit laid down or falling from the beam. She must therefore be familiar with how points can be deducted from her score whether they are connected with her movements or not.

Deductions. As with the other apparatus, the competitive gymnast must be aware of the penalties she may incur during a beam routine.

1. Fall on the floor or on the beam: 0·50.

2. Support with the hands on the beam to maintain balance: 0·50.

3. Support of a leg against the side of the beam: 0·20.

4. Poor head position during entire exercise: 0·30.

5. Coach present on podium during exercise: 0·50.

6. Coach signals gymnast: 0·20.

7. Monotony of rhythm in part: each 0.10.

Below: Familiarity with and confidence in working on the narrow platform of the beam must be the gymnast's first aim.

8. Monotony during the whole exercise: up to 0·40.
9. One full turn (360°) or large leap missing: each 0·10.
10. Monotony in the direction of movement: up to 0·20.
11. Domination of acrobatics: up to 0·20.
12. Linking movements not corresponding to difficulty level: up to 0·20.
13. More than three pauses: each 0·10.
14. All acrobatic elements executed in one direction: 0·20.
15. Too few links between gymnastic and acrobatic elements: up to 0·20.
16. Insufficient change of movements near and far from the beam: 0·10.

All these rules and deductions are laid down in the *Code of Points* by the FIG.

Below: Gesture, expression, movement— these must harmonize as naturally and smoothly as possible.

Training

In body preparation for beam work, the gymnast must aim to acquire suppleness, strength and spring. These qualities are, of course, among those she needs for the other apparatus. But now the gymnast also needs balance.

It has been noted that it takes courage for the young gymnast to perform on a narrow platform chest-high above the ground. Therefore the first skill that the gymnast should acquire in beam activity is that of becoming used to moving on the beam. This means spending a great deal of time first of all walking, then running, and then turning and jumping on the beam. But no-one expects the gymnast to begin her beam training on the high beam. In ideal conditions she will have the use of a low beam. If there is no low beam available, a bench such as those used in schools can be used, particularly for skills involving rolls, cartwheels and handstands.

One very important point about training for the beam is to remember that all skills should be first learned at floor level. Then and only then should the gymnast perform them on the low beam before moving to a higher beam. The gymnast's coach will make sure that whatever beam is used there are adequate mats under the beam during training and that practising new skills is adequately supervised. It is sometimes helpful to the coach if the gymnast wears trousers as this gives the coach something to hold on to.

The gymnast must realize that such training takes a long time. But she must also realize that, in the long run, the time will have been well spent — which takes us back to the initial practice, getting used to the beam and moving with confidence and control. Even walking must be controlled. The gymnast must concentrate on her posture, keeping her head up and her back straight. She should study pictures of well-known gymnastics stars to see how they hold themselves during beam exercises. Watch, too, the top performers in major competitions. See how they walk elegantly, with arms positioned to match their movements. The gymnast must be prepared to practise, practise and practise, if she intends to master the beam with any competence.

Once the gymnast has learned to walk on the beam and turn on her toes at the end of the beam, she can begin to practise running steps in the same manner. Rhythm and pace can be varied, once the gymnast can execute a basic run, and dance steps included. Remember to vary the turns by position of the body and by position on the beam. For example, turns can be performed while kneeling, squatting or sitting; and the gymnast can turn not just at the end of the beam but in the middle as well, proceeding backwards or forwards.

All training should include elements of a routine as specified in the *Code of Points.* Thus it is useful for the gymnast to tackle mounting and dismounting at an early stage. A good tip for learning beam mounts and dismounts is to practise them on a box horse before trying them on the beam. Two examples are the forward roll mount and the handstand mount.

Below: Training for the beam can be carried out on other equipment such as the box horse or school bench.

Full turn on one leg, free leg above 90°

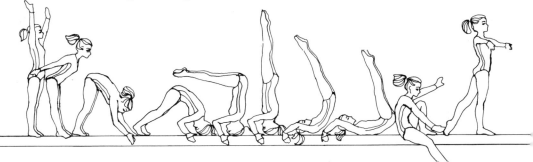

Forward roll

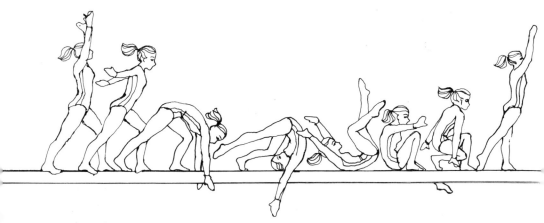

Free forward roll

Forward roll mount. Once a gymnast has practised a forward roll on a bench, she should try jumping up from a springboard to forward roll on a box horse. She must remember to 'land' on one leg as there is no room on the beam for two.

Handstand mount. In the same way, a handstand mount can be practised. When two boxes are placed end to end, the gymnast can move from the handstand into a roll, turn or forward walkover along the tops of the boxes. The move to handstand from the springboard can be varied, too: the gymnast can straddle or pike up.

Two box horses placed end to end can be used, too, for practising dismounts such as the round off dismount.

Below: Many movements on the beam can be practised on the floor or on a bench or box horse before being transferred to the beam.

Cartwheel

Back walkover

Round off dismount. The gymnast goes through a cartwheel on the end of the beam but in the handstand position turns facing the direction of travel so that she completes the landing facing the beam.

Other examples of mounts and dismounts are given below. For the remainder of the routine, the gymnast should assemble elements as outlined in the section on composition. She will be able to perform many of these movements from her training for the floor exercise. Essential parts of the beam exercise are jumps, hops, and leaps: these should be varied and practised on the floor first. Examples of leaps are stride leaps, split leaps, stag leaps, cat leaps, scissors leaps, side straddle jumps. Many other movements in the floor exercise can be used in the gymnast's beam routine; this will depend on how well she has mastered them 'on the ground'. As with the floor exercise, the gymnast and her coach must search for a routine which is fluent in performance and heightened with original links. Once more we come back to the word *balance*. The beam demands balance in performance, balance in content.

Once the gymnast has composed her routine, she must practise it constantly. An advanced gymnast expects to spend at least an hour going over her exercise or polishing up skills which she has not yet perfected. And while on the subject of skills, there is one that the wise gymnast will not neglect — the art of falling to the floor from the height of the beam. There is always a risk of injury if the gymnast does not learn to fall properly.

Below: The dismount off the beam is the climax of the exercise and can be a spectacular movement. The sensible gymnast will not, however, tackle any dismount outside her own skills and experience.

Opposite: A steady, confident dismount is a mark of good beam routine in a competition — from club level up to international standard.

The grouping of movements on the beam for scoring purposes are:

Mounts, Leaps, Stands, Body waves, Turns, Walkover — Cartwheels, Rolls, Handstands and Dismounts.

Below are examples of elements which the gymnast will find useful in preparing a competition routine.

List of movements

Two-legged squat mount.
Straddle mount.
Straddle over mount.
Squat on mount.
Y-scale.
Arched stand.
Arabesque.
Forward body wave.

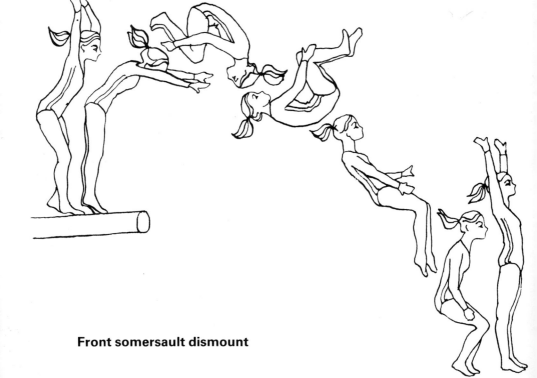

Front somersault dismount

Full turn on one leg, free leg above 90°.
Forward roll.
Backward roll.
Free forward roll.
Handstand roll.
Cartwheel.
Free cartwheel.
Back walkover.
Forward walkover.
Aerial walkover.
Handspring.
Back flip.
Back tucked somersault.
Free walkover dismount.
Handstand ¼ turn dismount.
Front somersault dismount.
Back tucked somersault dismount.

Back somersault dismount

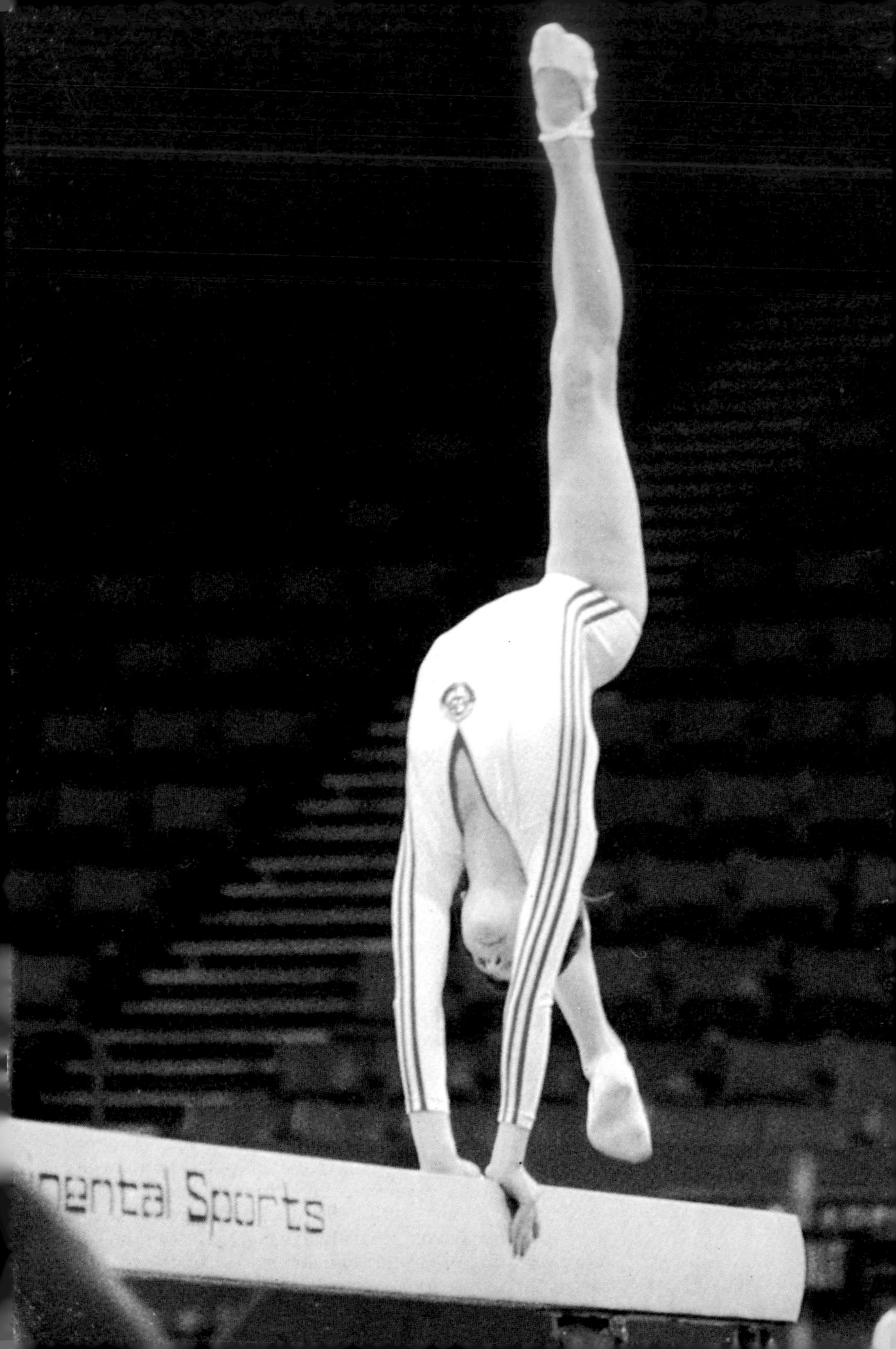
nental Sports

Above: Mary Lou Retton demonstrates relaxed balance control on the beam.

Opposite: Maria Filatova demonstrates a backward walkover on the beam. This well-known Soviet gymnast has the nickname of 'Masha'.

Finally, once the gymnast has acquired confidence, poise and ability on the beam, she must remember that the beam is a medium of expression. In other words, she must perform as her true self; not as an automaton or puppet. The great performers on the beam hold their audiences spellbound not merely by agility. They project themselves so that their personalities provide the final touch in a sequence more related to art than to sport. From them, the young gymnast can learn to approach her beam routine in a relaxed and tranquil manner. It is particularly important that she does not show tension in her face. The answer is, as always in gymnastics, to be in complete control of one's movements through thorough and painstaking preparation.

CHAPTER 7

COMPETITIONS

Whether the gymnast has reached the end of her gymnastics career or has just started it, her training is intended to help her compete to the best of her ability. At club or international level, she should aim for success by understanding the challenge of competition and the tactics required to meet it.

To all enthusiastic followers of gymnastics, the great moments in the sport are seen in competitions. Be it of international standard or a small contest held by the local gym club, a gymnastics competition can promise moments of drama, excitement and sheer beauty. It is the culmination of hard and sustained effort by the competitors and their coaches.

There comes a moment in every keen gymnast's life when she is ready to enter a competition. That moment will occur when she has made careful preparations through exercises to develop suppleness, strength and stamina. She will have also learned basic skills thoroughly and have acquired confidence, poise and grace in her gymnastics performance. Only when her coach or teacher feels that the standard of her work meets that set by competitions with which the club is involved, will she be encouraged to enter the next stage of her gymnastics career — that of being a competitor.

It is very likely that the first competition in which the gymnast takes part is one held within the club. It may well be a small one, with gymnasts competing on just two pieces — the floor and vault. There are usually two

reasons for this. First, many new clubs do not have the use of all the apparatus. Second, young gymnasts will have started their basic training learning floor and vault skills. The level of competition must clearly parallel the progress of the individual gymnast. In the lower levels of gymnastics, the gymnast will compete within her own age group for obvious reasons. Some leading gymnastics clubs will hold club championships to the highest possible standards, even conducting them in the same way as international competitions. Such competitions will include, of course, all four pieces of women's apparatus.

Outside the club, the budding gymnast will probably take part in an inter-club competition. Beyond that lie area and regional competitions. In the USA, every club has to belong to the United States Gymnastics Federation if they wish to hold USGF competitions in their state, but there are many clubs which do not. There is also the United States Association of Independent Gymnastics Clubs which has many members and which also holds gymnastics competitions. Leading clubs such as Kips and Parkettes hold tourna-

Above: At the age of 14, Nadia Comaneci of Romania won the top gymnastics competition, the Olympic Games. While she won the combined exercises title, however, the Soviet Union retained the team title they had held since their entry into the Games in 1952.

ments which attract competitors from far and wide. Success in a regional championship can lead to the gymnast taking part in a national competition or championships. The main USFG championships are the Junior Olympics, and the US and American Classics from which the best 12 girl gymnasts enter for the Championships of the USA, the national championships of the USGF. Success for a gymnast in a major competition could mean her selection for a national squad where she would train with other talented gymnasts for possible inclusion as an international team member. This would mean visits abroad to international matches and tournaments. The most prestigious competitions in the sport are the World Championships and the Olympic Games. The former is entirely devoted to gymnastics; the latter is a battle between countries which have qualified to send teams and individual gymnasts to the Games. The World Championships are held every two years, and are now arranged preceding and following the Olympics.

The ambition of every top class gymnast is to take part in both these outstanding contests. The Olympics, particularly, gains a great deal of international television coverage, and it is through this that gymnasts become known all over the world.

There may be a wide gap in standards between club competitions and those of international gymnastics, but participants in both must have the same aims. These can be summed up as preparation, practice, performance and perfection.

Preparation. No competent gymnast ever appears in a competition without spending considerable time preparing for it. Here she will need the help of her coach or club and she will need to concentrate on many details. Some may seem obvious, but it is surprising at times how many gymnasts forget important items until the last moment. Here is an elementary check list.

1. Find out about the competition. The gymnast and her coach or teacher must be familiar with the structure of the competition, any special rules involved and, if there are sets or compulsory exercises to perform, what these are. In the case of a compulsory floor exercise, music will be involved and the club must obtain the correct tape recording. Compulsory exercises for major competitions are published well in time for gymnasts to learn them. These are usually obtained through the gymnast's national federation.

2. Enter the competition in good time. If an entry or acceptance form has to be completed and returned, make sure that this is done speedily. Certain competitions require the competitors to become members of an association such as the BAGA or ESGA. There is a small

fee for membership on an annual basis and this must be paid before the competition.

3. Check the place and time of the event. Where is the competition going to be held? When does it begin? How long will it take — an afternoon, a day, two days or more?. All these points need to be thought of and checked. Expenses will have to be considered as well. Some competitions entitle the coach and her gymnast to travelling and accommodation expenses; others do not. Care must be taken, incidentally, where payment of expenses is concerned, that there is no risk that the amateur status of the gymnast is threatened. If there is any doubt, check with the national federation.

4. All clothing and equipment must be in first-class condition. Handguards, gymnastics slippers, leotards etc. — everything the gymnast uses must be in good order. Items must be checked for wear before the competition and not at the last moment. Any item that may affect the gymnast's performance adversely must be replaced or a spare provided.

Below: All over the world, vaulting practice is a familiar activity in leading clubs. Among leading clubs in the USA are Karolyi's Gymnastics where Olympic champion Mary Lou Retton trains, and SCATS where several international gymnasts are based.

Practice. Once a gymnast has found out the details of the competition, she can plan her routines accordingly. With compulsory exercises, she follows the movements laid down; with voluntary or free exercises, she and her coach must create routines that enable her to demonstrate every gymnastic and artistic talent she has. At the same time, the elements of her routines must fulfil the requirements specified by the competition rules and the *Code of Points*. Previous sections of this book have shown examples of movements needed for each apparatus and the gymnast should take care that her routines contain the correct balance of difficulty and type of element.

Having established the content of her routines (including her vaults and their numbers), the gymnast must now devote time to practising them. She must first learn them so that she can perform without hesitation, and she must also concentrate on perfecting each routine so that it becomes one continuous artistic expression. This calls for continual practice right up to the day of the competition. Great performers in other sports and arts have to do just that before they appear in public. The gymnast who does take her competition practice seriously

Below: The choice of music can make or mar a floor routine. That is why a gymnast is fortunate if she can call on the services of an understanding pianist.

has a better chance of doing well and obviously the more she puts into it, the better the results will be.

For some gymnasts, practising sets or compulsory exercises is the most tedious of activities. In a big competition, all the competitors will be performing exactly the same movements and this sense of repetition can be tedious to someone who enjoys the freedom of the voluntary exercise. Good performances in compulsory exercises, however, can make a vital difference to the result of a competition. In some major international fixtures, there is a team championship, an individual all-round competition and individual apparatus finals. In the Men's Team Championship of the 1978 World Championships, the importance of performing compulsory exercises well was dramatically proved. Favourites to win this section were the Soviet Union; their closest rivals, the Japanese, were much older. However, the 'elderly' Japanese gymnasts had learned their sets much more thoroughly than the Russians had. This fact, in the event, enabled the Japanese to clinch a narrow victory. Moral: learn your set exercises properly and do not underestimate their importance and value.

Below: Former world champion Nelli Kim was a formidable floor exercise competitor. She was Olympic floor champion twice — in 1976 and 1980 — and was also world floor champion in 1978.

Below left: During her career, Nelli Kim made regular trips to perform in London where she was highly popular with British fans.

Judges mark compulsory exercises on all four apparatus out of ten points. Deductions are usually included with the description of each exercise together with the time limit for the floor and beam exercises. If the gymnast leaves out a superior difficulty, she will be penalized 0·60 points; for omitting a medium difficulty, 0·30 points. The gymnast is allowed some freedom in the compulsory exercise in that she may reverse it totally or in part. But she may not change direction; otherwise 0·20 points will be deducted. She can also add or leave out two steps when reversing a movement on beam or floor.

The scoring for voluntary exercises, with the exception of the vault, is more complex, but it is highly important that the competitor understands it because it has a bearing on the planning of content and subsequent practice and performance. Each exercise is marked out of ten points.

Difficulty	5·00
Bonus points	
Originality, risk, C-part	0·50
Combination	
Distribution of elements	0·50
Composition	1·00
Space and direction	0·60
Tempo and rhythm	0·40
Execution and virtuosity	4·00
	10·00

Below: The scoreboard is unable to show that Competitor No 73 scored 10·00 on the asymmetric bars so it indicates 1·00 instead. The occasion was the 1976 Olympic Games in Montreal and the competitor was Nadia Comaneci.

Opposite: Mary Lou Retton of the United States waves to the audience as her vaulting score is announced.

The gymnast can now see why equal care should be given to the way she performs her voluntary routines as well as their content. She should remember this when she undertakes training for a competition.

Examining the composition of an exercise, the judges are particularly interested in the following factors.

As stated before, the *Code of Points* requires a voluntary routine to include difficulties as specified for certain competitions. There are three competitions for voluntary exercises in major international events and the difficulties required for each are these:

Competition 1B	Competition 2	Competition 3
6 A	4 A	2 A
3 B	4 B	2 B
1 C	1 C	3 C

The judges will not only make sure that each exercise is made up correctly of the right difficulties but that they are performed as a smooth harmonious whole. Every gymnast should search for new and interesting ways to connect her movements; success will reward her.

The judges will also look for variety; thus the gymnast must not be boring in her routines. She must vary her speed, the type of move, her direction. She and her coach must check that her routines are never repetitive or lacking in pace. The competent execution of an exercise is also very much part of its performance, so this aspect will be considered in the following section.

Below: Top Soviet gymnasts train for floor exercises by learning a group routine. This can form the basis of a display outside a competition.

Opposite: The floor exercise can be the climax of a competition. At the same time, a gymnast can enjoy its performance totally, having completed her routines on the other apparatus.

Above: Olga Korbut not only took the world by storm when she appeared at the Munich Olympic Games in 1972, she also performed a back somersault on the beam. This feat was considered by many to be highly dangerous. Olga won a gold medal for her beam work at Munich and although she achieved a higher score at Montreal four years later, could only come second in the individual beam exercise behind Nadia Comaneci.

Two tips for training on beam: while waiting to perform put cotton wool in the ears to deaden noise because sound is important in maintaining balance, and when the wool is removed, the gymnast may find it easier to work on the beam. Train in the same slippers as are to be used for competitions. That way, the gymnast will not be put off balance by a different 'feel' to the beam which unfamiliar slippers might give her.

Performance. Since half the marks of a voluntary exercise are based on the way that a gymnast performs it, she who wishes to give a top performance must be aware of what the judges look for in the execution of an exercise. The key word is *amplitude,* which has a very special meaning in gymnastics. It means full or wide, or abundant. Thus amplitude in gymnastics terms means that every movement performed by the gymnast must be fully and completely expressed — be they basic moves, jumps, turns, swings and so on. In other words, the gymnast must put her whole being into her performance; when she does so, she is more likely to produce an exercise which forms a

Continental Sports

complete artistic expression and is thus worthy of a good score.

Earlier, the gymnast was asked to consider what general impression implied. In scoring, it is worth a full point. One interesting definition of general impression has been made by Carol Leidke, the American international judge, and it is worth remembering.

This category involves the ease and beauty of the movement, manner, co-ordination, poise, rhythm, radiance, security, good posture, suitability of the exercise to the girl, neatness and appearance, performance with expression, grace, dynamic movement, use of hands and head, presentation, and the overall feeling expressed by the gymnast.

When the competitive gymnast takes the trouble to create the most favourable impression she can, she will be significantly distinguished from her opponents and this will be reflected in the scores given to her by the judges.

Above: Elena Davydova never reached the heights of fame that Olga Korbut did, but her feat of becoming overall Olympic champion in 1980 put her on a higher level of achievement than Olga.

The gymnast has four judges to impress in a big competition. These four are under the control of a master judge and are assigned to one of the apparatus. She is given the signal, usually a green light or flag, to begin her exercise by the master judge. The four judges mark the exercise out of ten points and each sends his or her score to the master judge. The master judge eliminates the highest and lowest scores, adds the middle two and averages these out to obtain the gymnast's score. For example, if the two middle scores are 9·0 and 9·2, the gymnast's score is 9·1. The master judge has to see that limits for differences in the marks are followed, as well as also producing a score for the gymnast which is used only in a dispute. Other judges, who do not mark, act either as timekeepers or ensure that gymnasts work within the limits and areas laid down for the apparatus.

During any of her routines, set or voluntary, the gymnast may fall and thus be penalized. It is therefore worth remembering the deductions set out in the *Code of Points*.

Fall from the apparatus: 0·50.
Fall during the dismount: 0·50.
Steps and hops: 0·10 to 0·20.
Fall on the knees: 0·50.
Fall on the seat: 0·50.
Support with one or two hands: 0·50.
Slight touch with one or two hands: 0·30.
Fall against the apparatus: 0·50.

If the gymnast falls at the end of the exercise and misses the dismount: 0·50.
If the missing dismount counts as a difficulty, there is a further deduction in the case of a superior difficulty: 0·60.
In the case of a medium difficulty: 0·40.

Opposite: Kathy Johnson of the United States demonstrates agility and poise to the judges in her graceful floor routine.

Below: Elena Davydova forfeits 0.50 points by falling. A list of deductions which a gymnast can incur during a competition can be found in the *Code of Points*.

When the day of the competition arrives, the gymnast should make sure that she is rested and relaxed. She must try not to perform in an overtired state. She should also eat lightly, with her last meal three hours before the competition. After she has reported to the competition officials, she should study the apparatus and note if they differ from those on which she has trained, or if she has more or less room to work on them than she is used to. For example, some gymnasiums have a shorter run up to the vault than others and the gymnast may have to adjust her run accordingly. She should hand in her tape recording of her music for the floor exercise to the right official. This, of course, must be marked clearly with her name. If the officials have special instructions for the competitors, the gymnast must listen clearly and follow them.

The gymnast must aim to arrive in time so that she can warm up carefully, ensuring that all her muscles are ready for competition. It is vital to warm up the body completely. The gymnast must see that her hair and her face look their best and that clothing and limbs are clean. If the gymnasium is brightly lit, a little make-up will

Below: Vera Caslavska, the famous Czech competitor, won seven Olympic gold medals and four silver. Her most outstanding achievement was at the Mexico Olympic Games in 1968 when she won four gold medals and a silver.

improve the appearance of the complexion.

Before and after each performance, the gymnast must present herself to the master judge at the apparatus. Between these two presentations, the gymnast is on her own, performing to show her love of the sport and how hard she has worked to achieve the best possible routine. If the gymnast can show the judges by expression how much she is enjoying herself, if she shows confidence and vitality, if she can demonstrate mastery of all the moves in her routine as well as prime physical preparation, then she is well on the way to becoming a first-class performer.

When a gymnast knows that she has performed well, she has the satisfaction of knowing that she has succeeded in a sport which makes many demands in time and hard effort before producing its rewards. Once a girl has been a gymnast, however, she will never lose the posture, grace and radiance which, in some ways, are the top prizes for the dedication she has shown in her aim to achieve the highest standards possible.

One highly important factor of success in gymnastics

Below: Elena Naimushina, the Soviet star from Siberia, came second to Nadia Comaneci at the *Daily Mirror* Champions All event in 1979 and received a well-deserved silver medal.

is the mental approach, first to the sport and then to competitions. A gymnast may be talented and skilled but she is hardly likely to perform well under the strain of a competition if her body and mind do not act in harmony.

So being a successful gymnast must start outside the gym, at home, at school, in whatever way of life the gymnast has. She must aim to be a 'complete' person; she must learn to enjoy every activity she does and try to make each action worthwhile. The gymnast must also learn to relax and at the same time be conscientious about matters such as grooming, eating the right food and keeping fit - all good for her morale. She must be interested at all times in the world around her and not shut herself off from the thoughts, ideas and influence of her friends, teachers and family. And as with her training, the gymnast must feel that she can improve on everything she does.

Below and opposite: While gymnastics demands total concentration from the gymnast, she must try and relax during moments when she is not working – in competition or in training. Here, three Soviet gymnasts relax during training for the 1979 *Daily Mirror* Soviet Display in London : Ilona Yarans (below) and Natalia Shaposhnikova and Svetlana Agapova.

When it comes to competition work, Boris Shaklin, the former Soviet Olympic star, has some good advice: *Only the gymnast who knows how to control his or her excitement and how not to go to pieces after the first failure can tackle competitions well.* What Shaklin means is that if the gymnast makes a mistake during a routine, she should carry on and complete the exercise to the best of her ability. She must not give up. She is bound to receive some kind of mark and she could score high marks on the other apparatus. In the same way, the gymnast must never be afraid of strong competition from other experienced gymnasts. She must remember that it is the final score which counts. Disregard the old saying, *for want of a nail, the battle was lost.* This does not apply in gymnastics.

The confidence of the gymnast can be boosted if she tries to experience the conditions of the competition a day or so before the actual event. For example, after warming up, she could attempt to carry out her whole competition programme with someone judging her on an

Below: Essential before every competition and training session : a gradual and thorough warm-up of the muscles. Having warmed up, the gymnast must make sure that she stays warm between her exercises.

unofficial basis. This creation of atmosphere is especially valuable when the gymnast is performing.

During the competition, the gymnast must try and relax before each piece, even if she only sits down for a moment. She should establish normal breathing and concentrate mentally on the rhythm of her routine, particularly on the performance of individual items and groups of actions. This mental concentration can be carried out at home, too. Shaklin says: *you must compose yourself for the performance of your first movements particularly carefully, because on these depends the subsequent progress of your programme. While you are performing each individual movement, give your attention not only to that, but also keep continuously in mind what comes next, so that not even the simplest movement leaves your mental control even for an instant. After all, mistakes and sometimes gross errors occur not only in the course of performing very complicated items but also in the performance of very simple ones. And this equally leads to low marks.*

Below: The gymnast should concentrate not only on performing the difficult moves of her routine but also on the simpler parts. This applies very much to the asymmetric bars. Mental concentration on routines can be carried out at home.

Above: During a competition, the gymnast is on her own. She may have the advice of her coach at hand but it is she alone who has to muster the willpower to take her through her exercises at peak performance.

Ten years ago, two American scientists — Doctors Bruce Ogilvie and Thomas Tutko of California State University — isolated eleven qualities which they considered to be the most important for athletes to have to be successful in competition. These qualities are interesting in that they can help the gymnast understand herself when she is assessing strengths and weaknesses in her personality with competitions in mind.

1. **Drive.** Desire to win or be successful.
2. **Aggressiveness.** Belief that one must be aggressive to win
3. **Determination.** Willingness to practise long and hard.
4. **Guilt-proneness.** Acceptance of responsibility for actions.
5. **Leadership.** Enjoyment of role as leader.
6. **Self-confidence.** Having confidence in self and abilities.
7. **Emotional control.** Tendency not to be easily upset.
8. **Mental toughness.** Acceptance of strong criticism without feeling hurt.
9. **Coachability.** Co-operation with coaches and teachers.

10. **Conscientiousness.** Possessing a sense of duty.
11. **Trust.** Acceptance of people at face value.

The gymnast and her coach can define these qualities further. There is a negative quality which is a very natural one for young gymnasts to have and that is fear. There are two sides to fear: one being related to performing on gymnastics apparatus and the other connected with the dread of performing in front of people at a competition. The former state can be lessened as the gymnast progresses in her training; the latter is again linked with experience, but needs a great deal of understanding by her coach at the time of her first competitions, to help overcome her apprehension. The gymnast must not hesitate to tell her coach if she is worried about any part of her training or competition work. One of the great benefits of gymnastics as a sport is that it helps many girls to overcome feelings of anxiety and timidity.

The gymnast must always be aware that her fellow-competitors are going through the same experience as she is. If she is mentally prepared as well as being physically prepared, she will have an advantage that will be reflected in her performances.

Above: Training and experience will help the gymnast overcome any fears about performing. She will gain confidence all the sooner with mental as well as physical preparation.

Perfection. The competing gymnast must have the determination to seek the highest standards possible and to keep to them. She must have that edge to her spirit which drives her on to improve her performances, competition after competition. She must be prepared to overcome tiredness and sometimes pain to give her best. If she does so, she will achieve tremendous satisfaction, win or lose, and, at the very least, the admiration of her coach, parents and club friends. So the first aim of the gymnast when she enters a competition is 'Nothing but the best'.

Below and opposite: Nelli Kim of the Soviet Union always sought perfection in her gymnastics and has, at times, achieved it. At the same time, she won the respect and admiration of fans all around the world.

GLOSSARY

AMPLITUDE Fullest extent to which a movement can be performed. Used as a standard of judging.

ARABESQUE A pose calling for balance common to dance and gymnastics. The gymnast stands on one leg with the other stretched back. One arm is extended upwards and the other arm sideways.

ARAB SPRING Also known as round-off. This is a version of the cartwheel, but is completed with the gymnast making a quarter turn from the vertical to land on her feet with her back to the direction of travel.

ASYMMETRIC BARS Second piece of apparatus in a women's gymnastics competition. Version of the men's parallel bars with the heights of the two bars varied to suit the strength of women.

BACK FLIP A back handspring.

B.A.G.A. British Amateur Gymnastics Association, the controlling body of gymnastics in Great Britain, comprised of regional associations and organizations with an interest in the sport.

BARANI A version of the aerial cartwheel or beam dismount performed without hands touching floor or beam.

BODY TENSION The control of muscles to hold the body firm without sagging during certain movements.

BRIDGE A basic movement when the body is arched backwards from a handstand with feet and hands on the floor.

CODE OF POINTS Book containing regulations governing the judging of gymnastics, published by the FIG.

BALANCE A static pose held briefly to demonstrate balance skill.

BALANCE BEAM Third piece of apparatus in a women's gymnastics competition. First developed in the last century to test balance ability. Only piece of apparatus designed simply for women.

COMPULSORY EXERCISES Also called set exercises. Published for all four pieces of apparatus before major competitions for competitors to learn and perform before the voluntary exercises.

DIFFICULTY Movement in the *Code of Points* rated as either 'easy', 'medium' or 'superior'

— A, B and C. A voluntary exercise, apart from the vault, must include a combination of difficulties. A C difficulty is worth 0·60 points, B 0·40, and an A difficulty 0·20.

DISLOCATION A grip on the asymmetric bars held while the gymnast hangs with her arms behind her back.

DISMOUNT The last movement in an asymmetric bars or beam exercise, when the gymnast jumps down from the apparatus.

ELEMENT A movement in an exercise.

F.I.G. Federation Internationale de Gymnastique, the world governing body of the sport. Based in Switzerland.

FLIC-FLAC A back handspring.

FLOOR EXERCISE The last exercise in a women's gymnastics competition performed on a 12m x 12m mat, involving dance, acrobatic and gymnastic movements. First women's floor exercise performed at the World Championships in 1952.

HANDGUARDS Straps made of leather, lamp wick or synthetic materials to protect the palms of the hands when performing on the asymmetric bars.

HANDSPRING A jump from feet to hands with a thrust to feet again and with the body moving in one direction.

HEADSPRING A movement where the gymnast places her head between her hands on the floor and thrusts while bringing her legs over to squat or stand.

HANG A basic position on the asymmetric bars where the gymnast hangs by her arms below a bar.

HECHT A dismount from the asymmetric bars and a vault in which the gymnast extends her arms sideways, keeping her body on an almost level plane before she lands.

HIP CIRCLE A circle around a bar in which the gymnast hold her hips close to the bar.

HORSE The item of apparatus on which gymnasts vault. In women's gymnastics, the horse is placed sideways.

JUDGE Four judges, supervised by a superior or master judge, mark gymnasts on each piece of apparatus in major competitions.

KIP Also upstart. A movement by which a gymnast

raises herself from a hang to a support position on a bar.

LAYOUT A straight and extended position of the body in vaulting, swinging or somersaulting.

LEOTARD One-piece garment worn by women gymnasts named after a nineteenth-century French acrobat.

MIXED GRIP A grip on a bar with both hands, with one palm facing the gymnast and the other facing away from her.

MODERN RHYTHMIC GYMNASTICS A recent development of Olympic gymnastics in which women perform with balls, ribbons, hoops, rope and clubs to music.

OLYMPIC GAMES The second most prestigious competition for gymnasts in the world. National teams must qualify at the previous World Championships for the limited number of places. However, the Olympics receive more television coverage and therefore more publicity than the World Championships.

PIKE A position when the gymnast folds or bends her body at the hips, keeping her legs straight.

PIROUETTE A full turn of the body when the gymnast is in a standing position.

PODIUM The raised platform or platforms in an arena where major gymnastics competitions take place and to which the gymnastics apparatus is fixed.

RADOCHLA A movement first performed by the East German gymnast Brigette Radochla which is basically a forward straddle somersault from the low bar to the high bar.

REGULAR GRIP The grip on a bar with both hands when the gymnast places her palms facing away from her.

REVERSE GRIP The palms of the hands face the gymnast when gripping the bar.

ROUND OFF See Arab spring.

ROUTINE The planned order of elements constituting a gymnast's exercise.

SALTO A full somersault without hand support.

SCORER Official at a competition who adds up the marks to find the results at the end of the competition.

SPLITS A movement, leap or pose in which the gymnast holds her legs in a straight line sideways or with either leg forwards.

SPRINGBOARD A springy piece of equipment used by gymnasts to give them greater height in vaulting or mounting apparatus.

STAG A leap or pose with one leg bent and the other held straight back.

SQUAT A movement when the gymnast bends her knees and hips while remaining upright.

STOOP When the gymnast leans forward or stoops as she vaults over the horse.

STRADDLE Basic movement when the gymnast holds her legs straight and apart.

SUPPORT A position when the gymnast supports her body on her hands with straight arms.

TSUKAHARA A well-known vault named after its Japanese originator. It is basically a cartwheel on to the horse followed by a one-and-a-half somersault off.

TRAMPETTE A small kind of trampoline used in gymnastics displays and sometimes for training.

TUCK A position in somersaulting when the knees are held to the chest.

UPRISE A swinging movement used by a gymnast to move from hang to support on the asymmetric bars.

TUMBLING A section of Sports Acrobatics which consists of somersaulting movements.

UPSTART See kip.

VAULT The opening piece in a women's gymnastics competition for which there are several kinds of vaults to perform.

VOLUNTARY EXERCISE In voluntary or free exercises, which follow compulsory exercises in a major competition, the gymnast may perform a routine of her choice provided regulations laid down by the *Code of Points* are observed.

WORLD CHAMPIONSHIPS The world's top gymnastics competition which takes place every two years. Open to all member countries of the FIG. See Olympic Games.

WORLD CUP A four-yearly major FIG event with invited competitors from member countries.

YAMASHITA A handspring vault with the body piking before landing, and named after its Japanese inventor.

INDEX

Pictures supplied by:

All-Sport 6, 11, 15, 21, 33, 42, 50-51, 61, 71, 80, 84-85, 88, 89,
    109, 124-125, 126, 127, 132, 135, 138, 140, 141, 148,
    149
Associated Sports 72, 73, endpapers
Astrid Publishing Consultants 3, 5, 16-17, 26, 27, 34-35, 43, 47, 49,
    56, 58, 66, 92, 95, 104, 105, 112, 113, 122, 129, 130, 131, 142, 143,
    144
Colorsport 56, 133, 139
Hulton Picture Library 13 (B), 14
Mansell Collection 9, 10, 12, 13 (T)
Leo Mason 123
Peter Moeller 8, 41, 67, 68-69, 83, 90, 93, 106-107, 119, 134, 136,
    137, 145, 146, 147
Artwork supplied by:
Astrid Publishing Consultants